John Florin Downey, Harvey Austin Fuller

Trimsharp's Account of himself

A Sketch of his Life - Together with a brief History of the Education of the Blind,

and their Achievements

John Florin Downey, Harvey Austin Fuller

Trimsharp's Account of himself
A Sketch of his Life - Together with a brief History of the Education of the Blind, and their Achievements

ISBN/EAN: 9783337157920

Printed in Europe, USA, Canada, Australia, Japan

Cover: Foto ©Raphael Reischuk / pixelio.de

More available books at **www.hansebooks.com**

TRIMSHARP'S

ACCOUNT OF HIMSELF:

A SKETCH OF HIS LIFE,

TOGETHER WITH A BRIEF HISTORY OF THE

EDUCATION OF THE BLIND,

AND THEIR ACHIEVEMENTS,

TO WHICH IS ADDED A

COLLECTION OF POEMS

COMPOSED BY HIMSELF

ANN ARBOR, MICH:

ANN ARBOR PRINTING AND PUBLISHING COMPANY.

1873.

PREFACE.

As I have, at the request of the author, read the following pages from the manuscript, for the purpose of preparing them for publication, it may be proper for me to state, briefly, the objects of the work.

Different authors have different objects in bringing their works before the public. With some it is a desire to become famous; with others it is to make money by the sale of the books; and with still others it is to impart knowledge and inculcate principles. The author of this work, who is no other than Harvey A. Fuller, B. S., the Blind Lecturer, will probably not feel injured if I say that he has all of these objects in view.

The first of these has not influenced him to a very great extent; though no doubt he partakes somewhat of the almost universal desire to be *known* and *felt*.

The second has had some weight; but all agree that to make money is a laudable object so long as people give "value received," and this the author has labored to do.

It is believed that those who read the book will realize that the third object, to impart useful knowledge and inculcate right principles, is attained.

There are but few men whose autobiographies people care to read; for a work of such a nature contains many details which, though interesting to the author himself, are very uninteresting to the public. But when one's career has been remarkable, or when it has been such that others may be benefitted by a statement of it, then his personal history becomes acceptable. For perseverance under difficulties, and for success in spite of one of the greatest misfortunes—that of total blindness—Mr. Fuller, the author of this little book, is certainly a rare example, and it is with the hope that those who are desponding and about to relinquish their efforts in despair may take heart and labor for excellence, that he sends this little volume abroad. Those who have seen his eager thirst for knowledge, who have seen him struggling, in poverty and darkness, for an education, until he completed a college course and graduated with college honors, who have seen him as a lecturer, winning honor to himself and entertaining and instructing hundreds of audiences, have felt that he possesses the sterling elements of a *man*, and that he is worthy of imitation.

Besides the principal events in the author's life, the book gives an account of the education of the blind, and of the achievements of notable blind persons. It also contains a brief sketch of Laura Bridgman, the deaf, dumb and blind girl, already somewhat familiarly known to the public, and an account of the ingenious manner in which she was instructed, the information being furnished mostly by the Superintendent's report and Dickens' Notes on American Travel. At the close will be found a number of the author's poems.

May the book be of interest and profit to the reader, and may the author, from whom the beautiful scenes of this world are forever shut out, realize that good time of Scriptural promise when "The eyes of the blind shall be opened."

J. F. D.

Ann Arbor, Mich., Nov. 20, 1872.

CONTENTS.

CHAPTER I.

POEMS.

TRIMSHARP'S ACCOUNT OF HIMSELF.

CHAPTER I.

WHENCE.

Murmur not, gentle reader, when I inform you that the name which stands at the head of this little volume is not the one I have generally borne and which I have endeavored to honor through my past life. For when I tell you that I came honestly by it, that it was the sole legacy of my lamented grandfather, who was an older if not a wiser man than the one who christened me, you will, undoubtedly, declare yourself in my favor and agree that, however appropriate or inappropriate it may be to my condition, I have a right to assume it if it suits my present purpose better than does the former one.

There are other mysteries connected with my history which, if thoroughly explained, would, no doubt, be made to appear equally clear and satisfactory. Then as a friend who loves you and feels a deep interest in your welfare, I advise that you compose yourself for a time and give me audience, while I shall relate, as well as I am able, some of the incidents connected with my birth and brief though eventful career in this mundane world of ours.

And first, permit me to say that my story shall be strictly true. " Truth is stranger than Fiction," and " Hon-

2

esty is the best Policy." I shall not falsify or color in the
least for the sake of making my life appear romantic,
brilliant or strange.

The first item I shall notice in this sketch, is the
time of my birth. For it does not seem to make so much
difference where a man is born, as the Proverb says, if he
is only born well. Though it was the constant regret of
a son of the Emerald Isle that he was not born in Dublin. He said he was born in Cork, though he might have
been born in Dublin had he chosen it, and if he were
ever born again, he would certainly be born in the latter
place. One of his reasons for this choice was, that while
potatoes could be obtained at Cork "free gratis," they
were much cheaper in Dublin. But to return; I was born
on Saturday evening, November 1st, year of our Lord
one thousand eight hundred and thirty-four. I am thus
particular in giving the date, in order to satisfy the minds
of some curious people who have manifested much interest in this matter, though I cannot say that I have
been prompted to write my book wholly on this account.
It is rather amusing, however, to observe the means
which some people who feel a little delicate about asking
an old Bachelor his age, resort to, that they may ascertain
this fact. Noticing that I have met with a slight misfortune (loss of sight) they first inquire, " At what age
did you become blind?" then, " How long have you
been so?" And by putting the two numbers together
they obtain the wished for information.

Of course I am not ashamed of my age. " Thirty-
four" was a good, productive year. My only regrets are,
first, that I had not been born in the spring that I might
have had a few months of growth and strength to pre-
pare me for the fierce blasts of our northern winter; and,
second, that I am not wiser than I am. But I do not

trouble myself much about these matters, for I am as stout as mankind in general; and when I reflect that there are many riding with me in the car of ignorance who have, if possible, received less advantage than myself, I pluck up courage and resolve to improve the present and future and let by-gones take care of themselves.

The next particular which it concerns you to know is the place of my nativity. Now I do think, after all, that it makes some difference where a man is born, be he born never so well. For instance, had I been born in ancient Jerusalem, I would, undoubtedly, have been a Jew. Had Rome been my birth-place, I probably should have been a Pagan. Had I been born in a Turkish harem, I should, no doubt, have been a Turk. Had New England produced me. I would, likely. have been a Republican. Had South Carolina had the honor, it might have made me a Ku Klux. But as it was. I was born of respectable parentage in the Empire State. at Mannsville, or two miles west of that place.

Having conducted you to the mansion in which I was born (a very respectable looking farm-house whose gothic roof points upwards so sharply as nearly to split the raindrops as they fall almost irreverently on its time-worn and moss-covered peak) we will now rest awhile and take a survey of the country. Yonder to the eastward beyond the little village of Mannsville (so called in honor of its founder, Mr. Mann,) extend as far as the eye can reach the hills and dales of Lorraine. Thickly covered. not with cedar and pines, like the vine-clad hills of Judea, which writers and speakers so often contrive to lug in whenever they wish to say something beautiful and have nothing else very beautiful to say, but with sturdy old hemlocks whose evergreen branches wave to and fro in the mazy autumnal breezes or the blasts of winter like giants

at a game of shuttle cock, affording both shelter and fuel to
those who require their aid. To make the place still more
desirable, stately groves of sugar maples, of fruited beeches
and of berry bushes send out a cordial invitation to all mankind to come and partake of the luxurious repast which
nature has so lavisly spread for them. Here the hum
of the busy bee may be heard as it gathers the nectar
from the fragant flowers, and here also may be heard the
ring of the woodman's axe, the crack of the sportsman's
rifle, the song of the mountain bird, the low growl of the
bear, the howling of the wolf, the fierce scream of the
panther and of the cat—all giving unmistakable evidence
that you are in the midst of animated existence. You
listen to the wild melodies of Nature, sung not as the
cultivated sing, but without stint or measure, without
being doled out to you by dint of coaxing—sung freely!
from Nature's orchestra within her own gorgeous temple.

But the crowning joy of all, and that which fills the
cup of happiness to overflowing, is the rosy cheeked girls
for which this country is justly celebrated. Their beauty,
attainments, and excellent habits excite the admiration
of the beaux of the adjoining districts and the rivalry of
their less fortunate sisters, who denominate them the
" Corn fed girls of Lorraine," for the simple reason that
they know how to make, and what is better, know how
to enjoy the good old-fashioned Rye and Indian bread
which our New England ancestors esteem so highly.

To the southward of us is a region of country called
Sandy Creek, and about five miles from where we are
standing is a pleasant little village bearing the name of
this town of which it is the metropolis, though it was
formally called Shavers' Corners by some facetious individuals who purchased their goods at this place. Hard
by this quiet hamlet is a silvery stream whose crystal

waters sport playfully over their pebbly bed, never ceasing their meanderings through glade and glen until they are lost in the bosom of mother ocean, though, to speak plainly, they are obliged to pass through Lake Ontario and down the River St. Lawrence before they can accomplish this.

Now if you will look toward the place where the evening sun is dipping his shining locks in the waters of the beautiful lake which skirts the golden horizon, you will behold an interval of country bearing the significant, though not very reverent, name of No-God. Its present inhabitants manifest some dislike to this name which their ancestors or some of their cotemporaries have bestowed on their country, so that a traveler passing through and inquiring the way to No-God, would be told all along the way that it was ahead of him until he nearly reached the lake shore, when he would be informed that he had left No-God many miles in his rear. But as no other appellation has been patented, we shall be obliged, for the present, to use the old name.

As this section is not unlike those already described, we will now turn our attention to the fourth and our last point of compass, Tory Hill. Whether this country received its name from the Tory weeds which grow so profusely over its stony surface or from the political sentiment of its inhabitants, I have not, after the most diligent research, been able to ascertain. A stranger passing over this country, would be reminded of the Yankee's description of his New England homestead, where he was obliged, he said, to grind the sheep's noses that they might reach the grass that grew between the stones. The present inhabitants of this section do not, as a general thing, partake of its nature, though a portion of them are inclined in this direction.

My grandfather performed once some missionary labor there. Now I do not mention the fact that my grandfather was a preacher out of any regard I have for family distinction. Minister's families are no better than others except as they sometimes receive better advantages, which was not particularly the case with ours. One of the sons, however, is a Minister quite eminent in his profession. Another son was born with the preach in him, but from some unaccountable reason it has never come out. His religious denomination, however, find him of great service. His argumentative faculties, his natural shrewdness, and his well cultivated organ of combativeness, render him an acceptable personage whenever any thelogical doctrines are to be discussed. On such occasions, if invited, he is always on hand, and always acquits himself so admirably that he satisfies his own party, satisfies his opponent and satisfies himself. Another son was born with equal genius, and while he was young, people thought that he was "cut out" for a preacher. They endeavored to encourage him in this direction by commending him at school and in other places for his attainments. But not being fond of flatteries, his indignation was aroused, and he determined to put an end to their talk as well as to defeat their plans for him. To accomplish this, he first resolved not to know any more than he was obliged to, and second, he resolved to recite his lessons wrong, although he knew them perfectly well, and in this way he was successful. He was, no doubt, "cut out" for a preacher, but spoiled in making up.

But I must pause a moment to wipe my eyes. Forgive these falling tears, but I cannot help sighing, not for my uncle alone, but for all mankind. Poor, frail, erring, suffering humanity ! How often have thy children come forth well born, designed for great ends, patterns of true excellence—but spoiled in making up.

We will now return to my grandfather, whom we left preaching to the people of Tory Hill. For a time he got on comfortably, but learning that some of the urchins improved the opportunity to play cards outside while he was preaching to the people within, he reproved the people, and insisted that this misdemeanor should be stopped. They being unable or unwilling to comply with his request, he gave them over to their own ways, and established himself in No-God where he was more successful. I judge this to be the case from the good Merino potatoes which were sent to our house from his parishioners. "By their fruits ye shall know them," has a significance in more ways than one.

But let us walk into the house, for I can now proceed with my narrative just as well in doors, and I see that you are shivering with cold. The November winds in this country are very severe, whether they come from the lake or some other quarter. Exposure to their blasts often produces colds, coughs, and consumptive diseases. I would not have you expose your health for the sake of listening to my story, especially since there is danger of taking cold myself.

I remarked that I was born of respectable parentage, and should I say more concerning this matter? Need I go on to inform you that my grandfather on my mother's side was a good, wise, and great man, a preacher, mechanic, and farmer, a man of Herculean strength, of indomitable will, and of unbounded sympathy? That his wife, my mother's mother, was a Christian woman, industrious and frugal, a loving wife, and a cherishing mother, and that my own dear mother inherited the good qualities of both? Or, crossing over

to the other ancestral line, shall I relate that my grand
father was a ship carpenter of good repute, poor in this
world's goods, but rich in the possession of a heart
always throbbing with generous impulse? That his wife,
my sainted grandmother, was a good, old-fashioned
Methodist woman, who shouted at prayer meetings and
labored prayerfully at home, and that, although her
sons stand aloof as if waiting for mankind and their
Heavenly Father to coax them a little, her daughters
enjoy the faith and love of good works which characterized their mother? Or going backward still further,
through the vista of wasted years, shall I trace my lineage
from Saxony to Britain, thence across the ocean in the
good old ship Mayflower, or some other vessel, to Plym-
outh rock, that mighty rock whereon poets and histori-
ans delight so much to dwell, (mentally, of course,
for no man could subsist on a rock, and this is only a
rock after all)?

All this, and much more, might be truthfully said.
But I forbear. It is not a history of my ancestors, but
a history (pardon my egotism) of myself that you desire, a history of Squire, Elder, Doctor, Professor, Lucifer,
Trimsharp, (I have borne each of these titles as man-
fully as I could) a man who appreciates kindness and
friendship to the highest extent, but despises hypocrisy
and falsehood, a man whose will-power, and never-flag-
ging perseverance have given him no little success in the
world, a man whose power of endurance, though not of
the best, is sufficient to enable him to hang out on the
wing, be his flight ever so high, or ever so low, until he
has finished his story.

But I notice by your sonorous breathing that you are
dozing. Do not be frightened; it is no breach of etiquette to doze a little when you cannot well avoid it. I

have been known to do this myself even at church; but I always tried to excuse myself, on the ground that the room was badly ventilated and the atmosphere too warm. But as you must be weary from the long march we've had you may go to rest if you like, and I will write the rest of my history. In a few days it will be finished and you can take it with you to read at your leisure. Meanwhile you will make yourself at home and enjoy life as best you can.

There are some rules of domestic etiquette which I would like to have visitors observe, but which many persistently ignore, by sitting up late at night and keeping others from their rest, and lying abed in the morning while the whole family wait for the guest to come to his breakfast. In a well regulated family such things are really distressing, especially if its members feel obliged to improve their time to the best advantage. But as you are a person of some experience in the world, your judgment and good sense will undoubtedly guide you in relation to these matters.

CHAPTER II.

Having given some account of my parentage, and described in a general way the old homestead where I was born, I am now prepared to enter upon the particulars of my own history. As my path of life has been more than ordinarily interspersed with thorns and roses, I shall be obliged frequently to change my tone of expression, giving place to both the serious and humorous incidents.

In the preceeding chapter, we have related nearly all that was necessary until we arrive at a point in our history where memory will furnish the needful material for our purpose. One event took place during this interval which I cannot forbear mentioning; it was the death of my mother, which occured when I was only six weeks old. Although unconscious at the time of the great loss I was suffering, I have since been made to realize to the fullest extent its effects upon my course of life. As others, more able than myself, have written much concerning a mother's love and influence, I shall attempt nothing in this direction. Suffice it to say that, when a mere child, I frequently found myself in tears when thinking of this bereavement, and was never able to see why it was that Providence should thus afflict me. But since I have become more experienced in the ways of the world and have felt, from time to time, the burdens of life pressing heavily upon me, I have concluded it was all for the best and have often wished that I, too, might find a resting place within that sequestered old burying ground.

At the time of my mother's death, she expressed a wish that I should be given in charge of my grand parents on my father's side, and her elder son, who was seven years my senior, should be left in care of her own family. This plan of my mother's was considered by the parties concerned as being the best that could be devised, and I was, accordingly, soon after her death, transferred to my new home, where I remained until nearly six years of age.

> " For I was wayward, bold, and wild,
> A self-willed imp—a grandame's child ;
> But, half a plague, and half a jest,
> Was still endured, beloved, caressed :
> For me, thus nurtured, dost thou ask
> The classic poet's well conned task ?
> Nay, Erskine, nay. On the wild hill
> Let the wild heathbell flourish still :
> Cherish the tulip, prune the vine ;
> But freely let the woodbine twine,
> And leave untrimmed the eglantine."

Being quite young at the time of this journey, I was permitted to take no observations on the way, but, on the other hand, was kept so closely confined within my wrappings that I could hardly breathe, and my cries for relief were choked by the frequent application of a large bottle to my lips. Whether this bottle contained milk or soothing syrup I am not able to state. Nor does it matter which, so far as my necessities were concerned, for I did not stand in need of food so often, nor was I so brilliant that I required drugging. But as it was, I was stuffed or dosed until I lost all consciousness of my condition until long after we reached our destination. (Note, this is not a record of memory. I observe that children are generally subjected to this kind of treatment, and so infer that I must have shared a similar fate.) The first event of my life that fixed itself indelibly upon my mind, transpired when I was between two and three years of age. One day a lady entered our apartments, and, after depositing her budgets on a table near the door, came to the place where I was seated, with her arms extended to receive me. I was no stickler for etiquette at that time more than I am at present. But I considered that such an action on the part of a stranger was unwarranted freedom if not a breach of hospitality, and so I protested against it with all the force I was master of until the lady's sense of propriety or my grandmother's interference caused the persecution to cease. Whether this affair had anything to do with the diffidence I felt for many years afterwards whenever brought into the presence of ladies, I will not assert; suffice it to say that if my fair friends have had reason to complain of my reserve or seeming indifference, they may attribute it in part to the imprudent action of one of their own number.

This grandmother, who was the principal guardian of the household, (my grandfather's business keeping him much from home) was the old-fashioned Methodist woman previously mentioned. She was not, however, a Methodist when she came to this country, but a member of the Close Communion Baptist Church. Finding in the vicinity of her new residence no organization of like faith, and wishing to gather around her some congenial spirits whose influence would aid her in Christian warfare, she united with the Methodist society, and remained in good fellowship with them until her death, which occurred many years afterwards.

This conduct of grandmother's will be considered by some as being reprehensible; but I see no necessity for such a conclusion. In the first place, she had not the advantages of a theological course. She had learned from her Bible that repentance, belief and baptism were the essential requisites to salvation, and, having complied with these and the duties enjoined in the gospel in relation to a public confession of the same, she then turned her attention to the elevation of herself and the elevation of others, both at home and abroad, supposing that no other burden was incumbent upon her. The Methodist principle of permitting their applicants for membership to accept of immersion instead of sprinkling, if their consciences dictated in that direction, settled all doctrinal questions in the old lady's mind, and she manifested on all occasions an equal love for both parties. In fact her mantle of charity spread itself over all religious bodies, and Satan himself might have put his head under it and kept it covered as long as he behaved well, by simply telling the old lady that he had made up his mind to lead a better life. And if you, my theological friends, who are so full of party spirit and party pride, would take a little stock in this charity institution and soften your hearts toward your heretical neighbors, remembering that they are your fellow beings, bound for the same eternal judgement-seat as yourself, you would gather around you many who, if not disposed to adopt your religious tenets, would, undoubtedly, listen to your kind instruction, and in Heaven bless you for the assistance you gave them.

Says T. DeWitt Talmage : " We have spent too much time in ecclesiastical pugilism. We have lost about a hundred years in gunning for Methodists, and drowning Baptists, and beating Presbyterians to death with the decrees, and pummeling Episcopalians with the butt-end of the liturgy. As at Bathwell Bridge the Scotch army quarreled among themselves, eighteen Ministers with eighteen different opinions. contending most fiercely.

until Lord Claverhouse came down with disciplined
troops and swept the field; so in the time when the
hosts of darkness in mail of hell were coming upon us,
we were contending, Old School against New School, Free-
Will Babtists against Close Communionists, Methodist
Church North against Methodist Church South, and we
have been routed on a hundred fields, when, forgetting
everything but the one-starred banner under which we
fought, and the Captain who led us on, we might have
shouted the victory through our Lord Jesus Christ. Thank
God that so many of the rams of the Church have had
their horns sawed off, and that the ecclesiastical chanti-
cleers have lost their spurs. The books of controversial-
ists will be on the shelves of College and State Libraries,
old and yellow and cobwebbed, until even the book
worms will get tired of the slumberous literature, and depart from old leather backs, and some day the books will
be cast into the fire, and just before the last flame goes
out, the world will see in the consuming scrolls the image of two religious combatants with their hands in each
other's hair, combing it the wrong way."

The example of my grandmother, so far, at least, as
preaching and praying were concerned, was so strictly
followed by me that much amusement was thereby created for those who visited us. One of this number was
a jolly old uncle who never left our house without en-
gaging me to pray for him, and paying me well for my
service. Whether he was prompted to do this solely because of the amusement it afforded him, or whether he
had some higher motive in view I am not informed (the
incident occuring too early in life to come within the
scope of memory). But I am told this matter was brought
to a termination in rather an amusing way. It is said
that one day while praying for him with all the fer-

vency the occasion demanded, I stopped suddenly and sprang to my feet exclaiming: "I see the Devil! I see the Devil!" and no reward was sufficient to induce me to undertake the ceremony for him again.

That Satan should visit me in my fancy is not strange, for my grandmother had given me a long history of his doings. She knew all his arts and allurements, and took great delight in recounting the victories she had obtained over him during her Christian warfare; and, being told by her that he inhabited the place where I should be obliged to go if I was not a good boy, of course I was interested in knowing all I could of him, and so I would frequently turn over the leaves of the old family Bible till I came to his profile, and then I would sit and gaze upon it with mingled feelings of pity and fear, for hours together.

I pitied him because he was chained so near that great fire that its heat must give him much uneasiness, and I could not bear to see even a mouse in misery. Then I feared him greatly; for he appeared a thousand times more dreadful than the ten-horned dragon of revelation now seems to be. In fact he must have resembled this symbol very much in general appearance, for he was a huge and terrible beast, with large eyes of liquid fire, and a mouth full of ponderous teeth. His four great claws seemed designed for tearing everything in pieces, while his long, forked tail was raised in air as if he were lashing his sides in great fury; and I actually feared that he might break loose from his moorings and come to this world, in which case I knew that he would do much damage before he could be chained again.

The vocation of my grandmother, aside from her domestic duties, was weaving. In this she greatly excelled, and when not employed in the manufacture of carpets

and cloths she wove window curtains of the rushes
which grew on the banks of the little stream that flowed
near our dwelling. These curtains were considered in the
days of plain living as being quite ornamental as well as
useful, and were readily purchased by the inhabitants of
the surrounding country. My grandmother, however,
found it necessary sometimes to carry these articles on
foot to the market places, which task she willingly performed. But before leaving home for this purpose she
would always invoke the assistance of the Lord, and
whenever a sale was made she regarded it as being the
work of Providence as much as though a kingdom had
fallen into her possession. I have a faint remembrance
of being with her on one of her pedestrian excursions.
Though I can not say whether she had any of her wares
with her or not. All I remember is our kneeling together by the side of a large log, and the impression
her prayer made upon me. When she had finished
she told me, by way of explanation, that she had been
praying for strength to pursue her journey, and she had
received it. She said, furthermore, that whenever we
needed anything we had only to pray and the good Lord
would willingly give it to us. I was very much pleased
with this information, and made use of it several times
afterwards as I may have occasion to show before finish-
ing this narrative. In fact, I admired the Lord so much
for his marvelous goodness that I became very anxious to
visit him, and accordingly promised my grandmother
that I would get a horse and carriage and take her to
Heaven as soon as I should be large enough to drive.

As my grandmother was dependent mainly on her
own earnings for our support, we did not, of course, live
in style equal to that of our wealthier neighbors. Still
we were comfortable and happy, and others who tarried

with us were made so. Among those who came of-
tenest to our home was a blind man, familiarly known
through Jefferson County as "Blind Jess." He was a
large, fleshy man, and gave as a reason for his obesity,
that he had the whole County to support him and why
should he not be fat? (Meaning by this that he was a
pauper). This allusion would have been to a sensitive
mind, inspired with the manly spirit of self-maintenance, truly humiliating; but Jesse had no such scru-
ples. Long familiarity with his condition had made
him reconciled to it, and he would have undoubtedly
remained at his charity home, contented and happy, had
it furnished him as many comforts as did the fireside of
the private families he visited. As it was, he used
frequently to steal out from his asylum and sojourn
among the people until some philanthropic individual,
prompted by the remuneration such services receive,
would carry him back. On one of these expeditions,
when he had got but a little way on his journey, he was
overtaken by one of the poor-house men, who invited him
to ride. As Jesse did not recognize his voice, he thought
it would be well to accept; but after a circuitous ride of
a few miles he was astonished to find himself again at
his old quarters. At this place the inmates were kept at
work as much of the time as their ability would permit,
and our blind friend found himself almost constantly
employed while there at turning grind-stone and doing
similar work which required strength and not eye-sight.
He was found very serviceable in the laundry; for as he
was quite strong, he could pound the clothes as well as
those who could see.

One day, while engaged at this business, a washer-
woman, for the sake of diversion, threw a pail of water
over him. Jesse waited patiently until she came round

3

to turn the clothes in his pounding barrel. Then he
seized her with one hand and with the other drew a wet
sheet from the barrel and wrapt it closely around her
head and shoulders. Her screams brought the overseer,
who, after inquiring into the matter, decided that Jesse
had done right, and told the girl that he hoped she
would meet with a similar fate whenever she attempted
to play such a game.

As this blind man had received no educational advantages, and possessed but little natural ability, he was
not, as may be supposed, a very interesting guest. Still,
he needed as much care and attention as though he had
been a prince or a preacher, and these were gladly
bestowed on him by my grandmother. Indeed, he used
to say that she was the only one who would have charity
for him, meaning by the term charity, faith in his visions.

In these visions, he claimed that he saw Angels or
" holy ones," as he called them, with bright, sunny faces
almost continually around him. When, however, he did
anything wrong, these visions would depart and not return
until he had thoroughly repented. During their absence,
he would appear dejected and taciturn ; but on their reappearance he would resume his natural cheerfulness and
loquacity. But these claims did not meet with the ap-
proval of those with whom he associated. They could not
see why he should be blessed with these special manifes-
tations of Divine favor more than themselves, and their
unbelief degenerated into a kind of ridicule or persecution.

Of course this feeling was not general, and the few
to whom it was confined would have been more con-
siderate had they stopped for a moment's reflection. If
the visions were imaginary they were certainly a high
order of imagination, and their possessor ought to have

been commended for keeping his thoughts in so pure a
channel; and if they were special revelations, there was
no cause for envy; for God, whose heart is ever touched
with the distresses of His children, has a right to manifest himself in a particular manner to one who, by his in-
firmities, is shut out from many privileges which others
of His children enjoy. But our friend has long since
gone to his rest, and if those who made sport of him,
or caused him to stumble, or neglected to warn him of
danger, ever get to that better world, or in sight of it,
they will see him there with his holy ones, gazing with
eyes of immortal vigor upon its resplendent glories, and
joining with the ransomed millions in the glad song of
eternal deliverance from all the cares and misfortunes
which temporal existence entails. Poor Jess! I do not
know why I have brought you into my narrative, unless
it is because in my retrospective glance I saw you groping your way along just as I did when a child, and
thought it would be a privilege to keep you company
until we arrive at a place where you could easily manage
yourself.

But the time has come for us to take leave of my
grandmother's cottage. It is the dearest place I have ever
known, and this is the reason why I have lingered so
long within its view. I am aware that "distance lends
enchantment to the scene," that, in the retrospect, we see
only the roses that are scattered along the path of life;
but, notwithstanding this, I do not hesitate to say that
the first six years of my life were, by far, the happiest I
have ever spent.

During this period my father had married again, and
settled in the west, and he and his new wife had concluded to take me to live with them. Accordingly they
wrote to my grandmother to this effect. As the world

had always been a Paradise to me, I thought that wherever I roamed I should find the same elysian fields, the
same sunny brooks, and the same tender hearts to care
for me, and, as the journey would afford me much diversion, I received the news with great pleasure. To add to
my anticipations, my step-mother promised to take good
care of me, and fill both of my pockets with sugar. This
I thought was extremely clever, and everywhere I went
I told my friends of my good fortune, and lauded the gen-
erosity of my new patron. I can almost hear, as I sit
dictating these lines, the merry laugh of my play-fellows,
as they saw me strutting up and down and stepping as far
as I could to show them how my step-mother did; for I
supposed that step-mother signified ability to stride
farther than other women.

But the hour for my departure arrived. My father
came and I was hurriedly prepared for the journey. I
could realize but little of the importance of what I was
doing; but my grandmother was greatly agitated. She
had taken me when I was a nursling, and had watched
over me for nearly six years—besides, she entertained
some fears for my future, and consequently would not
have consented to let me go had not the persuasions of
others induced her to place me in hands that were
stronger than hers, for my support. As it was, she
yielded up her claims, and with tearful eyes and falter-
ing voice she bade me good-bye. We had just crossed
the threshold, when my father, looking back and observing my grandmother's agony, remarked to her that if
she wished, he would not take me away. She made no
answer, but waved her hand for us to proceed. We
walked out to the carriage which was waiting at the gate,
seated ourselves within it and were soon afterwards
moving rapidly on our journey.

Thus ended my stay with the best friend I have ever found, or shall ever find in the realm of time. I have wished many times that my existence also had ended there; for since that time I have met with but little that was enjoyable, and with much that was hard to bear. Then, too, if I had died, Heaven would have received me; for my heart was almost as pure as the freest spirit that wings its flight around the sacred temple of the Eternal. But now I have learned many things which I must unlearn, I have formed habits of life, that must be overcome, and there are responsibilities resting on me, both in relation to my own improvement and to the improvement of others, which did not then exist. And in view of all these, I am frequently ready to yield up everything to the cruel demands of Giant Despair. Often, when gazing into the dark, untried hereafter, I see the Heavenly inheritance, with all its joys receding from my view, and, in its stead, a yawning gulf filled up with horrid shapes and figures loathsome to the sight open its ponderous jaws as if to make room for other victims to its savage lust. Sometimes I wonder if the Architect who framed the world would deign to bridge for me this awful void; but this I do not know. He's stern and unpropitious yet, and even earth itself is reeling now beneath my feet.

CHAPTER III.

After leaving Ellisburgh, we proceeded on our course, with little or no interruption, until we reached Oswego, where we left our private conveyance and took passage on a canal packet for Buffalo. In those times this mode of traveling was considered not only convenient, but quite expeditious (most of our railroads have been constructed since); and after a pleasant voyage of a few days, we arrived at our destination. Here we were soon afterward joined by my step-mother and her daughter Mary, a bright-eyed, flaxen-haired girl, about three years of age. And here I was subjected to an order of discipline quite different from that which I had before received. My step-mother, observing that I gave up everything to the demands of my little sister, threatened to whip me if I did not take my own part, adding that she could not bear to have a child around her who would not fight for himself. I believe she was not obliged to repeat this lesson many times for my benefit. Human nature, unrestrained by a higher power, very soon learns to take care of itself. I think, however, I have never been considered quarrelsome. When I am abused I take as little notice of the matter as possible, thinking that the ignorance or grossness which prompts such a course ought to be pitied rather than chastised. This philosophy corresponds with the story of the unfortunate lad who came within too close a proximity to

the heels of a fractious animal of the long-eared per-
suasion. He was disposed to overlook the offence after he
had considered its derivation.

But non-resistance was not the only virtue I lost
by my change of masters. Soon after we had crossed
lake Erie and traveled by land and canal to our new
home near Akron, Ohio, then a pleasant village and now
a city of some importance, I heard one of our neighbors
remarking to my step-mother that it was a rare thing to
find a child so truthful as myself, adding that his own
children would often tell a falsehood when the truth
would be much easier for them. This reputation, however, I was soon destined to lose, at least within our own
family circle. The circumstances which led to this de-
plorable result are as follows: My father was somewhat
irritable at times, the result, doubtless, of his dyspeptic
condition, and joined with this misfortune, for misfortunes never come singly, he was not very fond of children. As may be supposed, therefore, his conduct toward
me was not calculated to win my love nor scarcely my
respect for him. Then, too, the chastisings he occasionally gave me did not lessen the evil. I sometimes wished
he was dead, and often coveted the condition of the or-
phan children of my acquaintance, who I thought were
blessed, because they had no father to whip them. I was
never designed for rough treatment. I was fragile and
nervous, and what would have been a mere trifle for children in general seemed a horrid torture to me. Consequently I studied to avoid every infliction of punishment, whether of mental or of a physical character.

To accomplish this my first plan was to confess my
fault, and acknowledge that I desired retribution. But I
soon saw that this would not work. It seemed to justify
rather than nullify the action. Then I had recourse to

falsehood. This was more successful. It not only temporized the matter, but it often afforded permanent relief. Though, I think, on the whole, that the compunction of conscience I felt and the fear I entertained of being detected for days afterward, were more than any corporeal punishment would have been.

Now I do not wish to intimate that my father was heartless and cruel, for he was not. He lacked that which many others very much need, sound judgment or discretion. Had he chosen the weapon of moral suasion which my grandmother wielded so powerfully, he would, probably, have effected a thousand-fold more good than he could have hoped for with all his sprouts and horse-whips. Poor old man, he has lived to be quite aged, and I am thankful to say he has never received the whipping which I resolved so many times I would give him, and if his eyes ever rest on these lines, I hope that he will not infer from them that I cherish any ill feeling whatever. No, I long since forgave him for all the harm he did me, as freely as I hope to be forgiven.

My object in dictating this part of my narrative is, that those who have the care of children may be admonished. That some who read this may be led to study the different dispositions and temperaments of those who are intrusted to their care, and be induced to govern in accordance with them, is all that I wish or expect to achieve.

One virtue, if I may call it such, which my grandmother inculcated, lingered upon the threshold of my heart long after some of its kindred spirits had taken their flight. It was prayer. I continued this exercise, partly because I considered it a duty, and partly because of my belief in its efficacy. It may not be improper to introduce one or two circumstances here, as an illustration of my child-like confidence in God and in his willingness to answer me. I was returning home one dark night, and as a portion of my path lay through the woods, I was greatly concerned lest I might meet with some ghost or hobgoblin, for my mind had been filled with stories of these. As I was hurrying along as fast as my trembling limbs could bear me, I was suddenly stopped by the appearance of a hideous monster, directly in my path, who seemed to be waiting with out-stretched arms for my approach. What to do I could not tell. To advance would be death, to retreat would be to incur the displeasure of my father. I did not wait long, however, in this dilemma; for it flashed into my mind that God would protect me if I should ask his assistance. In a moment I was on my knees, and when I had finished my petition, I walked up to my supposed enemy (which was merely the top of a fallen tree), without any apprehension whatever. On another occasion, I was sent to bring the horses from the barn which was quite a distance from the house. My father and I generally harnessed them before breakfast, for I was not large enough to do it alone, and after they had eaten I would climb into the manger, put on their head-stalls and lead them out. At the time of which I speak one of the head-stalls was missing. I searched diligently for it, but it was nowhere to be found. If I called my father, he would probably whip me for my stupidity, and if I searched any longer, I should be corrected for my tardiness. These reflections caused my eyes to fill with tears; but suddenly it occurred to me that God knew where it was, and would tell me, if I prayed to him. I knelt upon the barn floor, and implored his assistance. When I opend my eyes after a brief prayer the missing article lay within my reach, and directly in front of me. Whether it had been miraculously placed there or not, I do not wish to say; but at the time I thought it was, and my faith was thereby strengthened.

A few months subsequent to my arrival at our western home, I was agreeably surprised by the addition of an infant brother to our family circle. I loved little Charlie (as they called him) dearly, and would often run nearly all the way from school to see him, my speed being generally hastened by the threats of a school girl older than myself who pretended that she was going to carry him away. A plague upon big girls, I thought; for there was another about the same age, whom they called "Beck," who used frequently to steal away with my hat, because she took pleasure in seeing me run after her. I suppose this was her object, for I think she was not large enough to have a real follower, though I do not know at what age girls are first inclined to accept the attentions of those indispensibles. (Here I discover that my amanuensis, a little girl, is laughing. I persume that such ignorance of human nature as I manifest ought to be laughed at.)

During the time I spent with my parents, which was about eight years, three other children were born to them, whom they named respectively Hattie, Alvin and Alber. One of these, my brother Alvin, died when he was quite young, and before I left home. He lived, however, long enough to deeply entwine himself into my affections. He was left almost wholly to my care, as he preferred me to the rest of the family, and when he died, it seemed as though a portion of my own existence was torn away. I stood by his bed-side holding his pale, thin hand, while his mild, earnest eyes looked imploringly into my own, as if he thought I could afford him some relief from his deep distress. But when I knew

that he was going, I left him to the care of others and
fled to an adjoining room ; for I could not bear to see the
Spoiler doing his last work on one I loved so much.
For many years afterwards I mourned his loss, and whenever I saw a child of the same age I would ask the privilege of holding it as long as circumstances and the
mother would permit.

When I had reached my fourteenth year, my parents
concluded to send me back to my native town. My father's
parents had moved to the West, and were then residing
in our vicinity ; but my mother's parents were still living
at the old homestead in Ellisburgh, and my parents,
thinking that they could do better for me than they
themselves could, decided to place me under their supervision. Accordingly a letter was addressed by them
to my grandfather stating their wishes, and upon receiving a favorable answer from him, they at once made prep-
arations for my journey. I was to go alone ; but this
did not seem to be taken into account by any of us,
though I now think I should be loth to send a child
thirteen years of age, who had never traveled except in
his infancy, on a voyage by canals and lake of five hundred miles, with scarcely money enough to pay his
passage.

We had never been destitute of the comforts of life ;
but sickness in the family, especially the illness of my father, had reduced our financial department to quite a low
ebb. I had managed to earn a little for myself from time
to time by voluntarily peddling molasses candy, by
catching fish for one of our neighbors, and by such other
means as were afforded me. But now I resolved to put
forth a greater effort, and on learning that the proprietor
of a ten-pin alley "down town" (for we were then living
in Akron) wanted boys to set up pins, I found him and

engaged in his service, where I remained about two weeks. I would have stayed longer, and been better prepared financially for my journey, but my parents did not like the company that I was keeping.

My step-mother thought that she could send me much cheaper by cooking my board for me. Accordingly, some bread and nice cakes were placed in my little old hair-covered trunk, with some hazel-nuts designed as a present for my grandparents, my wardrobe and a few trinkets, and I was ready to start.

The only hardship I had to encounter in this transaction, was the trial I experienced in parting with my friends, especially with my brothers and sisters. The youngest was not old enough to claim much of my attention but the others had been my constant companions for many years. Mary was now in her eleventh year. Charlie was eight, and Hattie was a little more than six years of age. The last named of these (little Hattie) seemed to appreciate the circumstance of my leaving home more than did any of the rest of us. She declared to the very last that she should go and stay with me at my grandfather's. I learned subsequently that she mourned my absence until her death, and was often found in the little closet up stairs weeping; and when inquired of as to the cause, she would always reply that she should never see Harvey again (this was my name in the family). Alas! her prediction was too true—but more of this bye and bye. I summoned up courage, and bade my father farewell; then I turned and said good-bye to the children, little thinking it was the last time I should see the little group, on earth. Then with my step-mother I proceeded to the packet landing, where we engaged my passage on a canalboat bound for Cleveland.

I observed, while my mother was talking with the

Captain about my going, that she was weeping, and when she came to take the farewell kiss she seemed to be almost as deeply grieved as if it was her own offspring who was going to leave her. She was naturally a kind-hearted woman, and, although she was at times rash and imprudent, I loved her dearly, and I yet believe I received the same care and discipline from her that she bestowed on her own.

The following day, we arrived at Cleveland. Here I was a little puzzled to know what course I should pursue. I knew that I was to cross the lake from this place to Buffalo; but which of the many vessels that thronged the harbor I was to take, or who among the busy crowd that surged up and down the streets and docks would give me any information, I did not know. My trunk was put ashore with other baggage, and thinking I had no time to lose, I picked it up and started in the direction of the shipping. I had not proceeded far, when I was accosted by a man who wished to carry my baggage. As it was quite heavy I consented to his proposition, and following closely behind him we threaded our way to the steamboat landing, where my guide, after taking pay for his services, disappeared, leaving me to my own reflections.

It was not long before a steamboat landed near the place where I was standing, and among the first who leaped upon shore was a man who called out that they were bound for Buffalo, and would carry cheaper than any other boat. I, with some others, followed him into a depot near by, and seeing him sell two or three tickets to a man for the voyage, purchased one for myself. I noticed on taking my ticket that it was not like the one which the man received; but I attributed this difference to the fact that the man was to have cabin fare, while I bargained for the steerage. To make sure of the matter, however, I went to the office on board of the boat and observed the tickets which they disbursed. Soon a large boy came up and bought a ticket for the same accommodation that I was to receive. On comparing mine with his I found they were not alike, and soon afterward I made my trouble known to some men who I knew by appearance belonged to the boat. They asked me who the pirate, as they called him, was, and, on my pointing him out, which I did with some difficulty, he having changed his coat, they went with me to seek redress. The agent of the boat (for such he was) acknowledged that he sold me the ticket and gave me another after making a little apology for his carelessness.

This affair created considerable sympathy for me among the boat hands, who soon became much interested in my welfare, and the interest was increased by a little circumstance which occurred soon afterwards. The large boy whom I have mentioned came around and the sailors, for the sake of diversion, asked us to wrestle with each other. I was not skilled in that art and the boy was nearly twice as large as myself, though he might not have been much older. But my heart was so full of gratitude that I could not refuse anything that was asked of me, and the boy being quite willing, we went at the work in good earnest. After a short struggle, I threw him forcibly upon the deck. The boy did not wish to renew the contest, and so, of course, I wore the victor's belt the rest of the passage. The sailors did not permit me to eat my own provisions but gave me warm meals with themselves and one of them gave up his berth and slept with a comrade, that I might have a comfortable bed. This was very fortunate for me, as the weather was extremely cold, and we were detained at Cleveland a day or two on account of the storm that was then prevailing.

My most particular friend on board was one of the engineers, whose name I have now forgotten. Through his kindness I was permitted to visit the engine room whenever I wished, a privilege I availed myself of very freely; for I took much delight in viewing the regular and powerful workings of the beautiful and ponderous machinery. This friend also gave me some information, which I considered at the time very valuable. He said the canal boats would transport me, free of charge, if I would work for them during the passage; accordingly, as soon as we landed at Buffalo, I took a brief survey of the city, and then went in search of such an opportunity. All the boats seemed to be full, but after walking some distance I found a Captain who was willing to take me. I thanked him for his kindness, and returned the favor as far as I was able by doing chores for him, and occasionally driving the team which towed the boat. All passed off well with me, but I think I was quite fortunate that I did not take the position of a hand, in which case my ignorance of canal life would have exposed me to iminent danger.

When we arrived at Syracuse, I took the stage for Mannsville, and soon after reaching that place found my way to my grandfather's home. Here I remained nearly three years, but nothing occurred in our vicinity during the time that would be worthy of record. Indeed, I look back upon that part of my life as being almost an entire blank, and, were it not for the acquaintances I made, who have since been firm friends to me, I should wish that this portion of my history were blotted forever from the pages of memory. My grandparents would have treated me kindly had they kept me under their supervision; but as they had become somewhat aged, they left the management of the farm and myself to their son

and his wife, who resided with them. These were so
eager to get rich (a thing which they never have accomplished) that they bore down everything before them;
and I, being artless and defenseless, went under with the
rest. Of course I have no malice in recording this matter, but merely place it as a monument of admonition.
God forgive me, if I cherish any hardness toward a being
that He has created, unless it be those spirits whom
He Himself cast out.

During the time I have just mentioned, an event occurred in my western home, which cast a gloom over
my rugged path. When I had been absent about two
years, I received a letter from my step-mother, informing
me of the death of three of her children, namely, Mary,
Hattie and Albert. The deaths of my sisters were both
occasioned by small-pox. Hattie passed away without
seeming to realize that she was dying, but Mary knew that
death was approaching, and made preparation for the
event. She gave directions concerning the disposal of
her little valuables, and even remembered me, although
I was at such a distance from her. I have in my possession the little book she left for me, and her last mes-
sage that I should meet her in Heaven shall never be forgotten. My sisters and some other children were exposed to this disease while at school from a boy who
came, ignorant, of course, of his condition, and the au-
thorities of the place, wishing to prevent its spread, or-
dered that those who died from its effects should be
buried in the night.

A few years afterwards I visited the graves of my little
brother and sisters and planted around them some
shrubs and flowers, then bade them good-bye with a hope
that the summoning notes of the Arch-angel shall bring
us together in a land where sorrows and misfortunes and
disease and death are unknown.

CHAPTER IV.

When I had reached my seventeenth year, I concluded to take another trip to the West. My parents had
written for me to come home, and my friends with whom
I resided gave their consent on condition that I should
wait until after harvest. My grandfather seemed reluctant to part with me, and offered me quite a sum if I
would remain; but I was tired of my situation, and
could not be prevailed upon to change my purpose. Accordingly, as soon as the time arrived, I drew my little old
trunk from its resting place in my bed-chamber, and,
after placing my few earthly possessions within it, and
receiving money enough to pay my passage, I bade farewell to my relatives and neighbors, and was soon afterward on my way rejoicing.

This time I traveled by railroad, with the exception
of a lake voyage from Buffalo to Cleveland, and a few
miles of stage ride from Hudson (Ohio) to Akron. It
was near midnight when I reached the end of my journey; but I was so anxious to see my parents and my
brother Charlie, that I set out at once in search of them,
although they resided at some distance from the stopping
place of the stage. I found their house without difficulty, although it was one they had built during my
absence; and my knock at the door was answered by my
step-mother, from her bed-room window, who wished to
know who I was and what I wanted. I replied that I

4

had come from Hudson that day, and would like to know where Mr. W—— (her brother) resided. She gave me the information, and retired; but as soon as I was convinced that she did not know me, I rapped again and upon her reappearance requested of her the privilege of staying the rest of the night, as it was so late. She gave her consent willingly, but soon after admitting me into the house gave warm tokens of recognition. The rest of the family were soon summoned, and our joy can be more easily imagined than described.

Immediately after my arrival I was sent to the village school; for, although my parents were uneducated, they earnestly desired that their children should receive all the advantages they were able to procure for them. I well remember the satisfaction they manifested on hearing from the Principal and Preceptress of the Akron Academy of my proficiency and good behavior, news which seemed rather surprising to myself; for, although I learned quite easily, I was generally too full of fun and too much disposed to take my liberty, to make very diligent application.

When I had been at home a few weeks, our family, myself included, visited my father's sister, who was then residing at Copley Center, several miles distant from our place. While at her house, my aunt proposed that I should stay with her through the winter, as she needed a chore-boy, and there was a good school near by. We all consented to this proposition without any reserve, except a little on my part, and I should have been highly elated at the prospect, for this was a favorite aunt, and my grandparents were living with her at that time; but I had purchased a violin with the intention of learning to play, and, knowing that my aunt was remarkable for her piety, strictness, and zeal, I feared she would not admit into her family so strange an innovation. I ventured, however, after a little hesitation, to make my objection known to her, which, to my surprise, she removed at once by saying that I might bring my instrument and practice all I desired. This indulgence she had just cause to regret many times before my stay with her was completed. Not that the violin was in any wise a stumbling block, for she had too much grace in her heart to be tempted into sin by any kind of music performed on any instrument whatever; but the horrid discords of an untuned old fiddle, when sawed upon by a novice in the art of music, must have been to the fine musical ear that she possessed excruciating beyond expression. She bore it, however, with a martyr-like spirit, never uttering a word of complaint, even when my exercises were the most ferocious and prolonged. I have always been grateful to her for the forbearance; not that my playing has amounted to anything of importance, but it kept me employed at home when my evenings would otherwise have been spent with the boys about town; and it is now, in my affliction, quite a comfort to be able to play a little for my own diversion and for the gratification of those around me.

When spring came, bringing with it cares and responsibilities, I began to look around me for something to do. As my parents did not need my services at home, it was decided, after some deliberation, that I should engage myself as cabin boy on some one of our lake steamers, if I could obtain such a berth. My step-mother's brother had for many years been master of a vessel, and it was thought he would be a good guardian for me. A letter was accordingly addressed to him, stating her wishes, and, provided with this, I set out to seek my fortune, urged on by the pecuniary reward I hoped my

services would command, and the pleasure I anticipated
from a life of travels. On my arrival at Cleveland I was
disappointed to find that my captain had retired from
the lakes, and after a brief but fruitless search for a similar opportunity, I returned to Akron, where I engaged
for a time in gardening and farm work for ourselves and
neighbors.

When the spring work was finished, I again set out
for Cleveland. This time I was as unsuccessful as before,
and was returning quite discouraged, when the captain
of a canal boat offered me a berth. It was not such a
position as I had expected; but as I needed the work, or
rather the pay for the work, I engaged in his service.
This boat belonged to the "Long Trade Line," as it was
technically called, which gave me an opportunity of viewing the country along the canal from Cleveland to Chilli-
cothe, a distance of more than two hundred miles southward from the former place.

After making a few trips, an opportunity for me to
visit another section of the country presented itself,
which I gladly accepted, partly because it would give
me a new field of discovery, and partly because the pecuniary inducements were much better. My new captain
took me, with some others, to Toledo, Ohio, and, after a
few days' preparation, we set sail for Lafayette, Indiana.
This canal is called the Wabash and Erie. It extends from Toledo to Evansville, a town in the southern
part of Indiana. It passes several towns of considerable
importance. Two of these in particular struck me as
being worthy of special notice, namely, Lafayette and
Terre Haute; the former, on account of its fine public
edifices and spacious dwellings; the latter, because of its
beautiful site and well-regulated streets. The soil of this
region is of a sandy nature, and, consequently, almost en-

tirely free from mud at all seasons of the year. But
the section near Toledo, known as the Maumee country,
is directly the opposite. There the roads are almost impassable, except when congealed by the frosts of winter,
or parched by the scorching rays of the summer sun.
And here, I am told, occurred the notable tragedy of the
man who had sunk to his crown in the mud. It is said
that a fellow traveller observing a hat lying on the ground
picked it up, when, to his surprise, he found it had been
covering a man's head. The man informed him that he
wished to be let alone, as he was perfectly able to take
care of himself, having, as he said, a good horse under him.

I had not been long in this country, when I was ap-
prised of the fact that those who came were expected to
endure a process of acclimation; in other words, they
were seized with a kind of disease known as the Maumee Fever, which attacked them soon after their arrival,
and generally bore them company during their stay. As
soon as this disease had fastened itself firmly upon me, I
was obliged to give up work, and go into the country for
recovery. I would have much preferred the small-pox,
dreadful as it is; for it visits a person but once, while
the other will dog his footsteps to the grave. I have
never known the small-pox, wicked and daring as it
is, to venture where this fever had obtained a foothold.
It sometimes infests these parts, but I think it always
sends out its scouts (chicken-pox and measles) in advance, to see if the coast is clear. This district has since
been drained of much of its stagnant water, which has
rendered it comparatively healthful. Still, the inhabitants feel obliged to keep constantly on hand, as an anti-
dote for this fever, a good supply of genuine whisky and
similar remedies.

When I was well enough to commence work again,
I hired to a farmer who lived near by, on condition that

I should labor for him the remainder of the fall, and do
his chores through the winter, for my schooling. Not a
very profitable arrangement, to be sure; but it was more
agreeable to my feelings than boating, which seemed at
that time to be my only alternative. This farmer, however, and his family, were respectable, and since my stay
with them have been among my firmest friends.

During my absence from home, a portion of my
family, before mentioned in this chapter, had removed
from Copley Center to Fremont, Indiana, and, as soon
as winter was over, they extended an invitation to me
to come and live with them, which I readily accepted.
They were at this time manufacturing wagons and car-
riages, and I was advised by them to learn the trade.
In fact, this was my principal object in visiting the place.
But after a few months of faithful trial, I was convinced
that I had not strength nor genius for the work, and so,
with the consent of my friends, I reluctantly gave up
the pursuit, but remained in that vicinity most of the
time until the following spring.

The intervening winter I look back upon as one
of the happiest seasons of my life. The old post-master
of the village gave me a home with him, and he and
his family used every effort to make my stay pleasant.
The school which I attended was taught by two of my
cousins, and, to make my cup of happiness still sweeter,
I was a general favorite with the girls and boys. At the
close of the winter term, I was informed by the principal
that I was well qualified for teaching; but as I knew of
no summer schools that would accept a young man for a
teacher, I did not take the trouble of obtaining a certifi-
cate.

After working a little around in the neighborhood, I
packed my wardrobe, with a New Testament which was a

present from my cousin, into my satchel, and set out in search of more permanent and profitable employment. On arriving at Toledo, O., I found a small steam tug which needed a pilot. I was not accustomed to the business, but shipped with the understanding that I should receive the necessary instruction. This boat was used for towing vessels up and down the river, and it was interesting to see with what giant strength she would lay hold on those large ships, often two or three at a time, and drag them to their destination. It was not long before I had learned the channel of the river, and acquired much skill in the management of the boat; and it gave me considerable satisfaction to know that my employers were well pleased with my success.

My pleasure, however, was not of long duration; for this was the season in which Toledo was visited with the cholera. Many of its inhabitants fell victims to this terrible scourge, and many others felt obliged to leave their homes and flee to the country for safety. Notwithstanding I was aware of the condition of things around me, I took no precaution whatever; but continued steadily at work, until I found myself suddenly prostrated under a severe attack of the disease.

As soon as its violence had subsided sufficiently to allow me to go to the country, I went to the home of my former friend, with whom I had lived the previous year, for rest and recovery. There I was taken with a relapse, which came near ending my days; but was soon recovered enough to walk around, and so concluded to return to my work. My friends were so much opposed to my going until I was more able, that I was obliged to steal away from them while my host was in the field, and, shortly afterwards, I was on the boat doing duty as before. This time, however, my labor was not so enjoyable as before my sickness. The weakened condition of my system induced a prolonged attack of ague and fever, which made it almost impossible for me to keep at work, especially during the chill. Often times I stood with my cold hands clutching the pilot wheel, when they felt and looked as if they were marked for the grave; and when a few minutes of respite were given me, I would go down with the furnace-man and stand near the melting fire until I was more comfortable.

I had proceeded in this way for two or three weeks, when it occurred to me I had better leave Toledo, and, thinking that a lake voyage would be beneficial, I engaged myself to the captain of a brig that was lying near by, to do his cabin work and cooking. I was not an adept in the art; but, with the instructions I had received at home and a book of recipes, I got on quite comfortably, and even received words of encouragement from some of my sailor friends, who seemed to have quite a propensity for eating. Our vessel was bound for Ogdensburg, New York, a port on the St. Lawrence River, and a few days after my coming on board we set sail for that place. It was my fate never to reach our destination; for, while passing through the ship canal that leads from Lake Erie to Ontario, I met with an accident which compelled me to leave the boat, and came very near compelling me to quit my hold on existence. While the vessel was lying in one of the deepest locks, waiting to be admitted to the channel below, I attempted to get on board by sliding down a large rope which extended from a snubbing-post of the lock down to the vessel's bow. I had no sooner placed my weight upon the rope, than it slacked down so suddenly that it caused me to lose my hold upon it, and I went head foremost into the water, many feet below. I was immediately aware of my imminent peril, but saw no way of escape. It was fortunate for me that the ship was not on the side of the lock to which it was fastened, else in my long fall I must have dashed my brains out upon the deck; but I knew that when it swayed back, as a vessel always does when the lock is being emptied of its water, I should be crushed between the wall and the vessel's side. While in this dangerous situation, I seemed to have a panoramic view of myself from my earliest remembrance up to that very moment when I was struggling for my existence. As I was an excellent swimmer, I soon came to the surface, observing which, our captain called out to one of the men to throw a rope to me; but the man was so excited by the circumstance that he looked all over the vessel for a detached piece, while there were hundreds of feet of coiled rope within his reach. He being the only man on board at the time, I was obliged to wait for him; but, as soon as he was able, he dropped a rope's end into the water, and, seizing it, I climbed to the deck, half dead with the exhaustion my effort and excitement had produced. I then went to my berth, and, after a few hours' rest, I came back to renew my duties; but I found that my place was occupied by another, and so concluded to take passage on a vessel that was bound for Toledo, with the intention of quitting the lake, for a season at least. On parting with my shipmates, I saw that they had been considerably affected by what had occurred. Some of them commended me for my dexterity in swimming; but others seemed to regard it as being of little consequence that my life was saved, as they thought by my looks that I had not long to live.

The captain and crew of the vessel on which I had taken passage treated me very kindly, as is their custom when any of their companions are sick or distressed.

After a few days of fine sailing, we reached our destination. By this time my health was somewhat improved,
and, thinking best to take another trip, I shipped on
board a schooner bound for Oswego, N. Y. This time I
was more fortunate than before; for I was able to perform duty until, on our return voyage, we had reached
Canada, when my strength failed, and I felt obliged to
take the railroad *en route* for Fremont, Indiana, hoping,
thereby, to obtain rest and recovery within the quiet circle of my relatives and neighbors. As my course lay
near the great Falls of Niagara, I concluded to visit that
place, and the few hours of extreme pleasure I experienced while there, richly repaid me for my trouble in
going. I found, however, that all persons are not so well
pleased with their journey to this popular resort; for a
friendly Irishman who bore me company on that occasion
was sadly disappointed. He thought that the Falls had
been misrepresented, and declared, many times over, that
they were a great humbug. He was finally quieted by
the retort of a lady to whom he had made this remark,
who replied, that if the river ran the other way over the
Falls, it would probably be some curiosity to him.

My journey to Fremont was not characterized by
anything unusual, except that my ghostly appearance
attracted the attention of my fellow-travelers, some of
whom remarked that I was a fair specimen of the workings of calomel on the human system. On my way I
called at Cleveland to receive my pay from the company
on whose vessel I had been sailing, and then went directly to my destination, and was soon afterwards enjoying
the hospitality of my friends.

My visit, however, was not so enjoyable as it had
been on previous occasions; for the fever still followed
me, and this, with the varied events of the past few

months, caused my naturally buoyant spirits to droop
themselves into the very dust. My aunt endeavored to
cheer me by saying that I would be better bye and bye,
and by telling me that I had succeeded far better than
many of those around me. Then, to particularize, she
mentioned the cases of some who were deeply distressed,
among others the people who were blind, and asked me
how I would feel were I deprived of sight. I replied that
I could not bear such a calamity, and should rid myself
of my existence at once.

Little did I know what I could endure when brought
to the task! Nor had I the remotest thought that, within
a few months, this bitterest cup would be pressed irre-
sistibly to my lips, until I had drank its contents to their
lowest depths, and thereby enkindled within me a flame
that should scorch and burn my soul into a state of mad-
ness bordering on desperation. People often assert what
they would do under such and such afflictions; but I
think that experience and observation warrant me in
saying that there is no condition in life so abject or de-
plorable, but that those who are plunged therein will
struggle for their existence as long as reason has sway.
In my childhood I received a fall which injured one of
my eyes to such an extent that afterwards it became
blind. The appearance of the eye was not much injured
by this accident; but I regarded the misfortune so deeply
that any allusion made to it would fill me with a sense
of pain or mortification. The other eye remained strong
and well most of the time until I was twenty years of
age, or a few weeks subsequent to my return to Fremont
from the lakes. After recovering a little from my illness
I began to assist my cousin in his blacksmith shop, and
was one day thus employed, when a hot cinder flew into
my eye which had before been injured. This caused a

burning sensation at the time, and there followed a severe
inflammation lasting many days. Shortly after this affair
I awoke one morning after a hard day's work, and found
my other eye so weak that I could scarcely see. My over-
exertion, combined with my ill health, had probably induced this weakness, and an inflammation ensued which
was heightened by frequent applications of severe medi-
cines prescribed by the village physician and others for
my relief. I continued in this state for many months,
suffering constantly the most excruciating pain, until,
finally, a severe cold destroyed my remaining sight. To
describe my feelings at this time would far exceed my
powers of delineation. Suffice it to say that, when I
found myself within this terrible darkness, I cursed my
existence and longed for death to relieve me. I envied
the lowest reptile that could see, and would have bartered
Heaven, with all its joys, for a little sight to guide me
through life's journey, could I have been assured that no
other punishment than annihilation should meet me at
its end.

In my most frenzied moments I imagined that God,
in his infinite mercy, could not punish a mortal so
afflicted for any course he might pursue, and, while
standing thus, clutching with a trembling hand the un-
sheathed dagger of suicide yet unstained, a thought came
to my mind that in some far-off Eastern city there might
be found a man of skill who could restore me, and, turning away, I resolved, weak and helpless as I was, to pursue at once this phantom of hope.

CHAPTER V.

As may be supposed from what has been stated concerning my stay at Fremont, the people there all knew of my distress and most of them gave me their warmest sympathy. Their sympathy, however, came to me indirectly; for I was not in a condition to hear anything from that direction, but studiously avoided the company of those who would be likely to offer me any condolence whatever. Another, and a far more substantial mode of expressing their feelings for me, was proposed several times, and was as often abandoned because of my disapproval. It was their earnest wish to circulate a subscription for my benefit; but I had always cherished a spirit of self-reliance, and was not prepared to receive any gifts, especially in a public way, and, consequently, replied to all their proposals, that I had earned means enough to defray my expenses until I should receive my sight, or until I should die, which I was confident would be a speedy alternative. It happened very fortunately for me at this time, that a neighbor and his family were about to visit the East, and, as they expressed a willingness that I should accompany them, I gladly accepted their kindness, and, by this means, found no difficulty in traveling. At Buffalo we obtained of an optician some eye-cups which he encouraged me to believe would restore my sight, but which I found, after a faithful trial, were as unavailing as the other remedies I had used. After receiving the cups I directed my course to Mannsville, thinking it would be best to visit my relatives until I should recover, or resolve upon some future course of action ; for, although I dreaded to return to my friends in such a forlorn condition, it seemed the best thing I could do, and I felt confident that they would give me a warm reception. In justice to these friends I will say that I was not disappointed in these expectations. There were residing in this vicinity several families of near relatives, and they vied with one another in doing all in their power for my comfort.

A few months subsequent to my arrival we were visited by a friend who was connected with the office of public instruction at Albany, N. Y. This friend was desirous that I should become a student at the Institution for the Blind in New York, and offered to secure an appointment for me, saying that I was entitled to a term of five years at that place. I readily consented to the plan, although my friends seemed very reluctant to part with me ; for I had in view, not only my education, but I trusted that something might be done for my eyes. As soon as I was installed in the Institution, I went to the eye infirmary to ascertain if there could be any thing done for me ; but was told by the faculty that my case was entirely hopeless. I then returned to the Institution, feeling gratified, indeed, to a sympathizing public for having established such an asylum, but too much weakened by sorrow and disease to avail myself of much of its benefits.

This Institution of learning, it may be proper to remark, was founded in 1832, and, at the time of my coming (1856), was located on Ninth Avenue between Thirty-third and Thirty-fourth Streets, the workshops being situated on Eight Avenue. The intermediate grounds were allotted to the students for recreation, the trees and shrubbery being no hinderance to their sports. The students at this time numbered one hundred and eighty, most of them being entirely blind. A few, however, had sufficient sight to conduct the others on the streets when they wished to go outside. These seeing ones formed the aristocracy of the place, though their honors were, of course, well earned. These blind students, strange as it may appear, were cheerful and happy and most of them were very talkative, seeming to take more delight in conversation than in meditation or study. Some of them, I noticed, were more loquacious and spoke louder when away from the Institution than at other times. This peculiarity may be attributed to their anxiety to be heard amid the noise and confusion of the streets through which they passed; but it often served as a roll-call to other blind friends, especially those of the opposite sex, who chanced to be within the sound of their voices; for chief among the regulations of the school was a law prohibiting the mingling of the sexes, and such plans as these were frequently devised in order to secure a friendly intercourse.

The blind seldom intermarry, though I have often found them enjoying the wedded life with those whose sight was imperfect, and, what seems strange to me, so far as my knowledge extends the children of the blind invariably possess good sight, although the parent may have been sightless from birth. There are many families of the blind thus situated, who support themselves by their trade, or by music, or as public teachers, who seem as comfortable and happy as those who see; and yet I believe that a majority of them would be in a better condition could they content themselves with a life of "single blessedness"—and this may be said with equal propriety of many who have the free use of their senses.

This Institution, like all those of the same character, had two departments of instruction; namely, Literary and Mechanical. The Literary Department comprised most of the English studies, and to these were added both Vocal and Instrumental Music. The instruction was given orally with the exception of Reading, Writing, Mathematics, and Geography, a knowledge of these being acquired by the sense of touch. The method of printing for the blind has been so often explained by others, that a description here seems quite unnecessary. The apparatus used in writing was simply a card in which were parallel grooves designed to guide the pencil, the student being previously taught the form of the letters by means of blocks carved for this purpose. In the study of mathematics a slate was used, which was so constructed as to receive type on which points representing figures were engraved. The maps used in this Institution were made of wood, the part representing land being elevated above that representing water. The mountains, boundary lines, cities and villages were indicated by slight elevations or pin heads, while the rivers were marked by small grooves. In the study of music, books with raised prints are sometimes employed; but, generally, the lessons are first read to the blind by a seeing teacher, and, when committed, can be easily taught by them to others. For any student of ordinary capacity to memorize a piece of music, only one or two readings are necessary. The blind can learn to play skillfully on all kinds of instruments, but the piano and organ seem best adapted to their condition. Many teachers and tuners of these instruments are employed in the city as well as the country and almost invariably give satisfaction. Indeed there is no barrier to the progress of the blind in any intellectual pursuit where a knowledge of color is not required.

Says S. G. Howe (Prin. of the New England Inst. for the Blind) under date of 1836, "There are many avenues open to the mind and, with the exception of color, all kinds of knowledge of the physical world may be obtained through the medium of other senses than sight.

"As to the mind, and all its powers, as to the moral world, and all its beauties, who cannot study them with his eyes closed or in his dark closet as well as in the broad blaze of day?

"For deaf mutes, we must invent a new language; and when it is afterwards perfected, still how imperfect is its range; how few of us learn it; and how like a man in a foreign country and ignorant of its language must a deaf mute ever be, among people who cannot talk to him by signs; yet to what beautiful and useful results have we arrived in the education of this unfortunate class!

" But how much broader is the avenue to the minds of the blind; how much nearer to us are they morally and intellectually; and how free, illimitable, and perfect may be our interchange of thought, reason, and feeling, by means of conversation and by reading!

" The deaf mute must ever carry his slate with him, as his imperfect interpreter. But the blind hears the lowest whisper and judges by the slightest intonation.

" To him, silence is a blackboard, on which every sound or tone writes its distinct and legible mark; and his ear signalizes, with unerring accuracy to his mind, every note in the gamut of feeling from the low breath of affection, to the stern accents of defiance.

" How much is lost by the deaf mutes in the dark or in the imperfect light of long evenings when their signs can be but imperfectly seen and understood; while the blind are ever prepared for conversation and exchange of thought.

"We know the world is full of bright and beautiful pictures. Now as we write, after having closed our eyes a moment to reflect upon the situation of the blind shut up in their dark cell of the body, when we turn toward the green grass and gorgeous blossoms in view, we feel a gush of inexpressible gratitude for the blessing of sight. Now can any one love better than we do to admire and adore the Power which gave beauty to the rose and lily, and its greater loveliness to the human eye and face when radiant with health, and feeling, and intellect? And yet, lovely and rich as is the world of sight, to us the world of sound is richer and lovelier; and should we be obliged to choose we would unhesitatingly prefer the darkness of the blind to the dreary solitude and unbroken silence of the deaf. We know there is a sudden shrinking at the thought of injury to the sigh and a shudder at contemplating the situation of the blind; but a little reflection and a little attention to the comparative advantages of each class would make all side with us. And to confirm this decision and show its wisdom, one has but to compare the blind and the deaf of his acquaintance and think who are the most cheerful, the most intelligent, and the most agreeable. It is only physically that the blind can possibly be considered as less favored than the deaf and dumb; morally and intellectually the advantage is immensely on their side; and their moral, religious and intellectual education is far more easy and may be far more advanced by art, than that of the deaf mutes.

" But, notwithstanding this truth and the apparent fact that their physical infirmity calls more loudly upon the community for aid in their behalf than in behalf of the deaf mutes who can learn a trade and gain a liveli-

hood, there have been comparatively few efforts made in
their behalf; and, until within a few years, our country,
which boasts of some of the first institutions in the world,
hardly knew that the blind could be taught in schools.
Within these four years, however, much has been done.
Already one of our institutions, at least, offers advantages for the intellectual education of the blind equal
to any in the world, and the others are rapidly acquiring
these."

Since the above was penned by Mr. Howe the work
has rapidly progressed until nearly every State of our
Union has its Institution for the education of the blind,
and by this means a class, hitherto helpless and dependent, are enabled to sustain themselves honorably and
comfortably in our midst.

We come now to speak of the mechanical department. In this several trades were vigorously and successfully pursued The manufacture of brooms and of
mattresses, being the most acceptable to the inmates of
the Institution, and chiefly sought by them. The ladies
of the Institution also received daily instruction in the
art of needle work, and displayed much taste and ingenuity in this direction. They threaded their needles
without difficulty and seemed to be quite proud of their
attainments.

The making of bead-work was conducted by the students independent of the Institution during the hours
allotted them for recreation, and the proceeds of their
labor brought them quite an income. Their wares consisted of wire and beads so arranged as to form card
baskets, vases, etc., combining the useful with the ornamental. The beads were put into boxes of different sizes
that their color might be distinguished. The idea so
often entertained that the blind can discern color by the

touch is true only as far as this, that the different coloring substances used for coloring purposes so affect the
fabrics as to render them easily distinguishable by the
sense of touch, color itself being intangible. The idea
of the blind in reference to color is that it compares
with the different varieties of sound—the darker colors
with the lower tones, while the brighter bear a relation
to the finer and higher keys. As an illustration, a blind
musician once said that red was like the sound of a bugle,
that scarlet resembled the music of the clarionet, and
green was like the ringing of bells.

Every Tuesday the Institution was opened for the inspection of the public. The visitors were conducted
through the different apartments by the blind graduates
who, in return, often obtained sales for their bead-work,
and sometimes received fine gifts or presents from the
most liberal of their guests. It was curious to note the
difference which existed in the minds of visitors with
reference to the ability of the blind; some supposing
that they could even paint the beautiful maps that hung
in the school room, while others wondered if they could
walk alone without stumbling or falling. Sometimes
they would converse about the blind in their presence as
though they considered them deprived of hearing as well
as sight. This of course afforded much amusement to the
unfortunates who were also often amused by the ludi-
crous questions that were often put to them.

One day, while a little boy was manufacturing a
large hand brush, a visitor inquired if he knew what
kind of a brush he was making and for what purpose.
The boy humorously replied that it was a tooth brush and
designed for cleaning the teeth. But the greatest curiosity
on the part of visitors was to know how they could eat un-
assisted, and frequently, during meal time, the windows

and doors of the dining hall were crowded with wondering spectators to witness this entertainment.

One day an individual who had never witnessed their skill at the table asked a blind boy to explain to him their manner of eating. The boy replied that he took a string and tied one end of it to the handle of a spoon and the other end to one of his teeth, then, filling the spoon with food, he traced the string up to his face, opened his mouth and tipped the spoon into it. Of course the stranger would infer there would be no further trouble in disposing of the food. For my own part, I can see no difficulty in the way of a blind person's finding his own mouth; but I remember an instance when a person of sight missed the mouth of another person, which he was trying to find. It is related of a miserly individual who, during the evening hours, would furnish no other light save that which came from the fire-place, that on one occasion, while taking his evening meal, a humorous fellow who sat near him thrust a spoonful of hot pudding into his (the miser's) face, remarking, at the same time, that it was so dark that he feared that he should get his mush into the wrong mouth. After this a light was never wanting, as Mr. Closefist did not relish hot mush in such profusion.

The students here, like those in seeing schools, were practical jokers. They did not, however, play their pranks so much upon their comrades as upon the new comers to the Institution. Generally, when a new student arrived, they would put a variety of questions to him and, being satisfied of his ability, position in society and depth of pocket (particularly the last, for money was quite a consideration with them, especially when in the hands of one who was liberally disposed), they would proceed to examine his qualifications for school.

First they would try his voice to see if he would do to enter the singing class; then he was required to dance, and if he did not move around quite as lively as they desired, they would request him to remove his boots and try it in his stocking feet, which he would do to the infinite amusement of the bystanders who stood gazing intently on the scene—with their ears of course. Sometimes it was seriously suggested that the student might receive his sight, and, being encouraged by this, he would willingly subject himself to the scrutinizing gaze of a blind man who, after a thorough examination, would declare his case a hopeless one. The results of these examinations were used during his stay as a reminder of his novitiate. As for myself, I escaped most of these trials; for when told by them that Holland had been taken by the Dutch, I replied that such jokes were stale with me and that they had better perpetrate them upon persons as verdant as themselves. This, with a few similar hits, gave me peace and a good reputation among them during the remainder of my stay.

We have already stated that there were nearly two hundred students at the Institution in the year 1856. This may seem an astonishing number to those who rarely meet with an individual of this class. But when compared with the thousands of sightless ones who grope their way in darkness over every habitable portion of our sunny earth, the number is, indeed, quite insignificant. As a few statistics in relation to the number of the blind may be acceptable to some of my readers I will here insert them, giving as my authority the American Encyclopedia and similar reliable works.

It is interesting to find that there is much less of this affliction in our temperate latitudes than in the ex-

tremely hot or cold climates; for instance, in the United
States the ratio of the blind to the entire population is
one to every two thousand three hundred and twenty-
eight, while in Egypt the ratio is one to every ninety-
seven.

In this country the ratio is also much less than in
Europe. The difference in the former case is attributable
to the fact that the sun's rays are more intense and daz-
zling when reflected from the polar snows and from the
glittering fields of sand in the torrid zone than when they
strike upon less reflective parts of the earth ; and, in the
latter case, to the facts that in the densely populated districts of Europe there are more accidents by gunpowder,
more prevalence of smallpox and other diseases which
often destroy the sight, and the intermarrying of relatives
is more frequent.

The number of blind in the United States is 10,000,
in Great Britain and Ireland 25,000, in Germany 30,000,
in France 33,000, in Russia 50,000, in the city of Yeddo
alone 36,000, and in the world the number exceeds
500,000.

Although there doubtless has been a large number of
this class in society from its earliest existence, or, at least,
so far remote as the time when the Patriarch declared
that he had been eyes for them, yet no public provision
was made for their education until the year 1780 when
Hany, a French philanthropist, established at Paris an
institution for their instruction. It is said that he was
moved in this direction while attending a blind concert
in which the performers were arrayed in peacocks' feath-
ers, donkeys' ears, and spectacles without glasses, designed
of course, as a burlesque. Hany, whose heart was keenly
alive to the sorrows of others, could not bear to see his
fellow beings thus subjected to ridicule, and so began at

once to devise means for their relief. His first student was a blind beggar to whom he paid a stipulated sum for his services. In a little time the student made such proficiency that others were induced to attend the school. A philanthropic society at Paris was also attracted to this object, and by their assistance the number of students was soon increased to twenty-four. In the year 1786 it was thought best to give an exhibition before the king, which was done with so much success that the king granted them an annuity.

Everything went on harmoniously with Hany and his *proteges* until the year 1791 when, France being plunged into a state of revolution, the government neglected to give them their support. The philanthropic society that had assisted them was obliged to withdraw its patronage as many of its members were in exile; and, being thus left in a destitute condition, the school was scarcely able to maintain its existence. It is said that Hany at this time lived on one meal a day for more than a year that his pupils might not starve.

When peace was restored the institution went on as prosperously as before, until the government concluded to unite this institution with another asylum of the blind which had existed in Paris for many years. The members of this asylum had never received any instruction in literature or in mechanics and were, therefore, indolent and vicious. Soon after this union it was discovered, as might be expected, that the example of those who were bred in idleness had a pernicious effect upon the students, and Hany who could not bear to see the fruits of seventeen years' labor thus despoiled gave up his situation and retired to private life. He did not, however, remain long in retirement as he soon received an invitation from the Czar of Russia to come to his dominions, which he accepted and shortly after founded an institution for the blind at St. Petersburg.

Dr. Howe, after describing Hany's career at Paris, says: "Among the first six of Hany's pupils, two attained eminence and are now living monuments of what may be done by the blind; one is Alexander Rodenbach, late member of the Belgian Representative Assembly, an ardent and intelligent patriot, a good speaker and an influential man; and the other is a Professor of Mathematics in the college at Angers. The fame of Hany's success in teaching the blind to read, write, cipher, etc., reached the ear of the Emperor of Russia, who invited him to come to St. Petersburg and establish an institution there. The direction, given for it, however, were much in the same spirit as would have been issued for a bear garden, or a Rarey show at which the people might wonder, and for which they might glorify the government. It was rather an attempt to make the people do wonderful things *tour de force* than to enable them to overcome the obstacles in the way to their improvement and independence. Accordingly the institution soon sank into insignificance and disappeared, while one at Berlin, established by some individuals on whom Hany engrafted his spirit, took deep root and is now flourishing. Other institutions were soon established in different cities on the Continent and in England. The best are those of Edinburgh, Paris, and Vienna. These institutions are of two kinds, some uniting intellectual education with instruction in the mechanical arts, others confining the pupils entirely to work, as weavers, basket makers, braiders, etc. Those of England are principally of the latter kind, at Liverpool, indeed, they are taught music and many churches are supplied with organists from the school for the blind. They are however not taught to read or write."

The school at Paris continued to decline until all their studies were abandoned with the exception of music, and this was chiefly performed by Hauy's old students. About twelve years subsequent to the resignation of Hauy, whose place was filled by an ignorant superintendent, the institution was separated from the old asylum that had encumbered it and a new superintendent chosen for the place. Unlike his immediate predecessor, the new comer was a man of energy and ability; but his efforts were directed mainly to his own aggrandizement and not to the welfare of those who were intrusted to his care. In order to effect his purpose more successfully he purchased manufactured articles from the shops of the seeing and exhibited them as the workmanship of his own pupils; he further taught them to recite lessons in Latin, Greek, German, Italian, and other languages, while at the same time they were ignorant of the most rudimentary examples in Arithmetic. His glory, however, was not of long duration; for the government officials, suspecting his course, entered into an investigation which resulted in his disgraceful dismissal from the institution. The superintendent who followed him was a man of virtuous character and fine achievements; but it was soon discovered that he had not a tact for educating the blind, and the position was given to one of the teachers who had been twenty-five years in their service. He was a man eminently qualified for the position, and under his supervision the institution soon gained an enviable and lasting reputation.

In a little less than fifty years from the time that Hauy, whom the French justly style the apostle for the blind, commenced his work of philanthropy at Paris, a similar movement was inaugurated in our own country by Dr. S. G. Howe, whom I have quoted so extensivly in this connection. The work was completed in the year 1832, and was located at Boston, Massachusetts, under the title of theNew England Institution for the Blind. This earnest philanthrophist, Dr. Howe, to whom the blind, of this country especially, are so much indebted for his untiring labors in their behalf during the past half century, is the same that instructed Laura Bridgman, the deaf and dumb and blind girl, with whose doings the public have been so long familiar. This child of misfortune was deprived from her earliest infancy. not only of her sight, hearing and speech, but mostly of the sense of taste and smell; yet, notwithstanding this seemingly impassable barrier, she has learned to do many things that are truly marvelous and has also obtained a knowledge of the moral world and its beauties, surpassed by few who live in the enjoyment of all their senses. Dr. Hoag, after a visit to the Boston Institution for the Blind where he met Miss Bridgman, says, " I have seen Laura Bridgman whom God sent into this world without sight, hearing or the power of speech. She could see nothing, hear nothing, ask nothing. To her the very thunder has ever been in silence, and the sun blackness. The tips of her fingers and the palms of her hands have been her eyes and tongue, yet that poor, sickly girl knows much of the earth, of language and numbers, of human relationship and passions, of what is, has been, shall be, should be. of sin. death and hell, of God, Christ and Heaven; and all this has gone darkly through that poor child's slender fingers, darkly feeling of the fingers of another, and thus she tells her hopes, fears and sorrows ; and if she, groping thus blindly for the Savior, finds him and rests her weary hands on his lowly head, that blessed head that bows lowly enough even for this, oh! how will she rise up in judgment and condemn you, O, sinner, upon whose soul every sense is flowing the knowledge of God, while your eyes read His holy word, and your ears hear a thousand times over those tidings of great joy, even the glorious gospel of the blessed God!"

During one of Ireland's severest scourges by famine Laura Bridgman is said to have earned with her own needle a barrel of flour, and sent it to the relief of those starving, helpless people. It is characteristic of those in the deepest affliction to be most solicitous for the welfare of those who are alike unfortunate; and, so far as duty is concerned, it makes little difference whether the enlightened soul inhabit a temple of health, sight and hearing, or whether it be pent up in that dark, silent tenement of which we have just spoken.

As many enquiries have been made respecting the mode of instruction pursued in educating Laura Bridgman, I will here insert some particulars which were given by Charles Dickens in his notes of American travel. He quotes from an account written by that one man who has made her what she is:

"'Laura Bridgman was born in Hanover, New Hampshire, on the twenty-first day of December, 1829. She is described as having been a very sprightly and pretty infant, with bright blue eyes. She was, however, so puny and feeble until she was a year and a half old, that her parents hardly hoped to rear her. She was subject to severe fits which seemed to rack her frame almost beyond her power of endurance, and life was held by the feeblest tenure; but when a year and a half old she seemed to rally, the dangerous symptoms subsided, and at twenty months old she was perfectly well.

"'Then her mental powers, hitherto stinted in their growth, rapidly developed themselves, and during the four months of health 'which she enjoyed, she appears (making due allowance for a fond mother's account) to have displayed a considerable degree of intelligence. But suddenly, she sickened again ; her disease raged with great violence during five weeks ; when her eyes and ears were inflamed, suppurated, and their contents were discharged. But though sight and hearing were gone forever, the poor child's sufferings were not ended. The fever raged during seven weeks, for five months she was kept in bed in a darkened room; it was a year before she could walk unsupported, and two years before she could sit up all day. It was now observed that her sense of smell was almost entirely destroyed, and consequently her taste was much blunted. It was not until after four years of age that the poor child's bodily health seemed restored, and she was able to enter upon her apprenticeship of life and the world.

"'But what a situation was hers ! The darkness and the silence of the tomb were around her ; no mother's smile called forth her answering smile, no father's voice taught her to imitate his sounds; they, brothers and sisters, were but forms of matter which resisted her touch, but which differed not from the furniture of the house, save in warmth, and in the power of locomotion ; and not even in these respects from the dog and cat. But the immortal spirit implanted within her could not die, nor be maimed nor mutilated, and though most of its avenues of communication with the world were cut off, it began to manifest itself through the others. As soon as she could walk she began to explore the room, and then the house ; she became familar with the form, density, weight and heat of every article she could lay her hands upon. She followed her mother and felt her hands and arms, as she was occupied about the house, and her disposition to imitate led her to repeat everything herself. She even learned to sew a little and to knit. The reader will scarcely need be told, however, that the opportunities of communicating with her were very, very limited, and that the moral effect of her wretched state soon began to appear. Those who cannot be enlightened by reason must be controlled by force, and this, coupled with her great privations, must soon have reduced her to a worse condition than the beasts that perish, but for timely and unhoped for aid.

"'At this time I was so fortunate as to hear of the child, and immediatly hastened to Hanover to see her. I found her with a well formed figure, a strongly marked, nervous-sanguine temperament, a large and beautifully shaped head, and the whole system in healthy action. The parents were easily induced to consent to her coming to Boston, and on the fourth of October, 1837, they brought her to the Massachusetts Asylum for the Blind at Boston. For a while she was much bewildered; and after waiting about two weeks, until she became acquainted with her new locality, and somewhat familiar, with the inmates, the attempt was made to give her knowcledge of arbitrary signs, by which she could interchange thoughts with others.

"'There was one of two ways to be adopted ; either to go on to build up a language of signs on the basis of the natural language which she had already commenced herself, or to teach her the purely arbitrary language in common use ; that is to give her a sign for every individual thing, or to give her a knowledge of letters by combination of which she might express her ideas of the existence and the mode and the condition of existence of

anything. The former would have been easy but very
ineffectual; the latter seemed very difficult, but if accomplished, very effectual. I determined to try the latter.

'"The first experiments were made by taking articles
in common use, such as knives, forks, spoons, keys, etc.,
and pasting upon them labels with their names printed in
raised letters. These she felt very carefully, and soon,
of course, distinguished that the crooked lines *spoon*, differed as much from the crooked lines *key*, as the spoon
differed from the key in form. Then small detached
labels, with the same words printed upon them, were put
into her hands, and she soon observed, that they were
similar to the ones pasted on the articles. She showed
her perception of this similarity, by laying the label *key*
upon the key, and the label *spoon* upon the spoon. She
was encouraged here by the natural sign of approbation,
patting on the head. The same process was then repeated with all the articles which she could handle, and she
very easily learned to place the proper labels upon them.
It was evident, however, that the intellectual exercise was
imitation and memory. She recollected that the label
book was placed upon a book, and she repeated the process first from imitation, next from memory, but apparently without the intellectual perception of any relation between things.

"'After a while, instead of labels, the individual letters
were given to her on detached bits of paper; they were
arranged side by side so as to spell b-o-o-k, k-e-y, etc.;
then, they were mixed up in a heap, and a sign was made
for her to arrange them herself, so as to express the words
b-o-o-k, k-e-y, etc., and she did so.

"'Hitherto the process had been mechanical, and the
success about as great as teaching a very knowing dog a
variety of tricks. The poor child had sat in mute amaze-

ment and patiently imitated everything her teacher did ; but now the truth began to flash upon her, her intelect began to work, she perceived that here was a way by which she could herself make up a sign of anything that was in her own mind and show it to another mind, and at once her countenance lighted up with a human expression ; it was no longer a dog, or a parrot, it was an immortal spirit, eagerly seizing upon a new link of union with other spirits. I could almost fix upon the moment when this truth dawned upon her mind, and spread its light over her countenance. I saw that the great obstacle was overcome, and that henceforward nothing but patient and persevering, but plain and straightforward efforts were to be used.

"'The result, thus far, is quickly related, and easily conceived ; but not so was the process ; for many weeks of apparently unprofitable labor were passed before it was effected. When it was said above, that a sign was made, it was intended to say that the action was performed by her teacher, she feeling his hands and then imitating the motion. The next step was to procure a set of metal types, with the different letters of the alphabet cast upon their ends, also a board, in which were square holes, into which holes she could set the types, so that the letters on their ends could alone be felt above the surface. Then, on any article being handed to her, for instance a pencil, or a watch, she would select the component letters and arrange them on her board, and read them with apparent pleasure. She was exercised for several weeks in this way, until her vocabulary became extensive, and then the important step was taken of teaching her how to represent the different letters by the position of her fingers, instead of the cumbrous apparatus of the board and types. She accomplished this speedily and easily, for her intellect had begun to work in aid of her teacher, and her progress was rapid. This was the period, about three months after she had commenced, that the first report of her case was made, in which it was stated that she had just learned the manual alphabet, as used by the deaf mutes, and it is a subject of delight and wonder to see how rapidly, correctly, and eagerly she goes on with her labors. Her teacher gives her a new object, for instance, a pencil,—first lets her examine it, and get an idea of its use, then teaches her how to spell it, by making the signs for the letters with her own fingers; the child grasps her hand, and feels her fingers, as the different letters are formed; she turns her head a little on one side like a person listening closely; her lips are apart; she seems scarcely to breathe; and her countenance, at first anxious, gradually changes to a smile, as she comprehends the lesson. She then holds up her tiny fingers, and spells the word in the manual alphabet; next she takes her types and arranges her letters; and last, to make sure she is right, she takes the whole of the types composing the word, and places them upon, or in contact with the pencil, or whatever the object may be.

"'The whole of the succeeding year was passed in gratifying her eager inquiries for the names of every object which she could possibly handle; in exercising her in the use of the manual alphabet; in extending in every possible way her knowledge of the physical relations of things; and in proper care of her health.

"'At the end of the year a report of her case was made, from which the following is an extract: 'It has been ascertained beyond the possibility of doubt, that she cannot see a ray of light, cannot hear the least sound,

and never exercises her sense of smell if she have any.
Thus her mind dwells in darkness and stillness, as profound as that of a closed tomb at midnight. Of beautiful
sights, and sweet sounds, and pleasant odors, she has no
conception; nevertheless she seems as happy and play-
ful as a bird or a lamb; and the employment of her intellectual faculties, or the acquirement of a new idea, gives
her a vivid pleasure, which is plainly marked in her ex-
pressive features. She never seems to repine, but has all
the buoyancy and gayety of childhood. She is fond of
fun and frolic, and when playing with the rest of the
children, her shrill laugh sounds loudest of the group.

"'When left alone, she seems very happy if she have
her knitting or sewing, and will busy herself for hours;
if she have no occupation, she evidently amuses herself
by imaginary dialogues, or by recalling past impressions;
she counts with her fingers, or spells out names of things
which she has recently learned in the manual alphabet
of the deaf mutes. In this lonely self-communion she
seems to reason, reflect, and argue; if she spells a word
wrong with the fingers of her right hand, she instantly
strikes it with her left, as her teacher does, in sign of disapprobation; if right, then she pats herself upon the
head and looks pleased. She sometimes purposely spells
a word wrong with the left hand, looks roguish for a
moment and laughs, and then with the right hand strikes
the left, as if to correct it.

"'During the year she has attained great dexterity
in the use of the manual alphabet of the deaf mutes, and
she spells out the words and sentences which she knows,
so fast and so deftly, that only those accustomed to this
language can follow with the eye the rapid motions of her
fingers. But wonderful as is the rapidity with which
she writes her thoughts upon the air, still more so is the

ease and accuracy with which she reads the words thus
written by another; grasping their hands in hers, and
following every movement of their fingers, as letter after
letter conveys its meaning to her mind. It is in this way
that she converses with her blind playmates, and nothing
can more forcibly show the power of mind in forcing
matter to its purpose than a meeting between them. For
if great talent and skill are necessary for two pantomimes
to paint their thoughts and feelings by the movements
of the body, and the expression of the countenance, how
much greater the difficulty when darkness shrouds them
both and the one can hear no sound.

"'When Laura is walking through a passage way with
her hands spread before her, she knows instantly every
one she meets, and passes them with a sign of recognition; but if it be a girl of her own age, and especially if
it be one of her favorites, there is instantly a bright smile
of recognition, and a twining of arms, a grasping of hands,
and a swift telegraphing upon the tiny fingers, whose
rapid evolutions convey the thoughts and feeling from
the outposts of one mind to those of the other. There
are questions and answers, exchanges of joy or
sorrow, there are kissings and partings, just as between
little children with all their senses.

"'During this year and six months after she had left
home, her mother came to visit her, and the scene of
their meeting was an interesting one. The mother stood
sometime gazing with overflowing eyes upon her unfortunate child who, all unconscious of her presence, was playing about the room. Presently Laura ran against her,
and at once began feeling her hands, examining her
dress, and trying to find out if she knew her; but not succeeding in this she turned away as from a stranger, and
the poor woman could not conceal the pang she felt at

finding that her beloved child did not know her. She
then gave Laura a string of beads which she used to
wear at home, which were recognized by the child at
once, who, with much joy, put them around her neck, and
sought me eagerly to say she understood the string was
from her home. The mother now tried to caress her, but
poor Laura repelled her, preferring to be with her acquaintances. Another article from home was now given
her, and she began to look much interested; she examined the stranger much closer, and gave me to understand
that she knew she came from Hanover; she even endured
her caresses, but would leave her with indifference at the
slightest signal. The distress of the mother was now
painful to behold; for, although she had feared that she
should not be recognized, the painful reality of being
treated with cold indifference by a darling child, was too
much for woman's nature to bear. After a while, on the
mother's taking hold of her again, a vague idea seemed
to flit across Laura's mind that this could not be a
stranger; she therefore felt her hands very eagerly, while
her countenance assumed an expression of intense interest. She became pale, and then suddenly red; hope
seemed struggling with doubt and anxiety, and never
were contending emotions more strongly painted upon
the human face; at this moment of painful uncertainty,
the mother drew her close to her side and kissed her
fondly, when at once the truth flashed upon the child,
and all mistrust and anxiety disappeared from her face,
as with an expression of exceeding joy she eagerly nestled
to the bosom of her parent, yielding herself to her fond
embraces.

"'After this the beads were all unheeded, the play-
things which were offered to her were utterly disregarded,
her playmates, for whom but a moment before, she had

gladly left the stranger, now vainly strove to pull her from her mother; and though she yielded her usual instantaneous obedience to my signal to follow me, it was evidently with painful reluctance. She clung close to me as if bewildered and fearful; and when, after a moment, I took her to her mother, she sprang to her arms, and clung to her with eager joy. The subsequent parting between them showed alike the affection, the intelligence and the resolution of the child. Laura accompanied her mother to the door, clinging close to her all the way, until they arrived at the threshold, where she paused, and felt around to ascertain who was near her. Perceiving the matron, of whom she is very fond, she grasped her with one hand, holding on convulsively to her mother with the other; and thus she stood for a moment, then she dropped her mother's hand, put her handkerchief to her eyes, and turning round clung sobbing to the matron; while her mother departed with emotions as deep as those of her child.

"'It has been remarked in former reports, that she can distinguish different degrees of intellect in others, and that she soon regarded almost with contempt a new-comer, when, after a few days, she discovered her weakness of mind. This unamiable part of her character has been more strongly developed during the past year. She chooses for her friends and companions those children who are intelligent and can talk best with her; and she evidently dislikes to be with those who are deficient in intellect, unless indeed, she can make them serve her purporses, which she is evidently inclined to do. She takes advantage of them, and makes them wait upon her, in a manner that she knows she could not exact of others; and in various ways she shows her saxon blood.

"'She is fond of having other children noticed and

caressed by the teachers and those whom she respects ; but this must not be carried too far, or she becomes jealous. She wants to have her share, which, if not the lion's, is the greater part ; and if she does not get it, she says, " my mother will love me."

" 'Her tendency to imitation is so strong, that it leads her to actions which must be entirely incomprehensible to her and which can give her no other pleasure than the gratification of an internal faculty. She has been known to sit for half an hour, holding a book before her sightless eyes, and moving her lips, as she has observed seeing people do when reading. She one day pretended that her doll was sick, and went through all the motions of tending it and giving it medicine ; she then put it carefully to bed, and placed a bottle of hot water to its feet, laughing all the time most heartily. When I came home she insisted upon my going to see it, and feel its pulse ; and when I told her to put a blister on its back, she seemed to enjoy it amazingly, and almost screamed with delight.

" 'Her social feelings, and her affections, are very strong ; and when she is sitting at work or at her studies, by the side of her little friends, she would break off from task every few moments, to hug and kiss them with an earnestness and warmth that is touching to behold. When left alone, she occupies and apparently amuses herself, and seems contented ; and so strong seems to be the natural tendency of thought to put on the garb of language, that she often soliloquizes in the finger language, slow and tedious as it is. But it is only when alone that she is quiet ; for, if she becomes sensible of the presence of any one near her, she is restless until she can sit close beside them, hold their hand and converse with them by signs.

"'In her intellectual character it is pleasing to observe an insatiable thirst for knowledge, and quick perception of the relations of things. In her moral character, it is beautiful to behold her continual gladness, her keen enjoyment of existence, her expanisve love, unhesitating confidence, her sympathy with suffering, her conscientiousness, truthfulness, and hopefulness.'

"'Such are a few fragments from the simple, but the most interesting and instructive history of Laura Bridgman. Her great benefactor and friend who writes it is Doctor Howe. There are not many persons, I hope and believe, who, after reading these passages, can ever hear that name with indifference.

"'A further account has been published by Dr. Howe since the report from which I just quoted. It describes her rapid mental growth and improvement during twelve months more, and brings her little history down to the last year. It is very remarkable that, as we dream in words, and carry on imaginary conversations, in which we speak both for ourselves and for the shadows who appear to us in those visions of the night, so she, having no words, uses her finger alphabet in her sleep; and it has been ascertained that when her slumber is broken, and is much disturbed by dreams, she expresses her thoughts in an irregular and confused manner on her fingers, just as we should murmur and mutter indistinctly, in the like circumstances.

"'I turned over the leaves of her diary, and found it written in a fair, legible, square hand, and expressed in terms which were quite intelligible. Without any explanation, on my saying that I would like to see her write again, the teacher who sat beside her, bade her, in their language, sign her name upon a slip of paper, twice or thrice. In doing so, I observed that she kept her left hand always touching and following up her right, in which, of course, she held the pen. No line was indicated by any contrivance, but she wrote straight and freely.

"'She had, until now, been quite unconscious of the presence of visitors; but having her hand placed in that of the gentleman who accompanied me, she immediately expressed his name upon her teacher's palm. Indeed her sense of touch is now so exquisite, that having been acquainted with a person once, she can recognize him or her, after almost any interval. This gentleman had been in her company, I believe, but very seldom, and certainly had not seen her for many months. My hand she rejected at once, as she does that of any man who is a stranger to her; but she retained my wife's with evident pleasure, kissed her, and examined her dress with a girl's curiosity and interest.

"'She was merry and cheerful, and showed much innocent playfulness in her intercourse with her teacher. Her delight on recognizing a favorite playmate and companion, herself a blind girl, who silently, and with an equal enjoyment of the coming surprise, took a seat beside her, was beautiful to witness. It elicited from her, at first, as other slight circumstances did twice or thrice during my visit, an uncouth noise, which was rather painful to hear. But on her teacher's touching her lips, she immediately desisted, and embraced her laughingly and affectionately.

"'Well may this gentleman call that a delightful moment in which some distant promise of her present state first gleamed upon the darkened mind of Laura Bridgman. Throughout his life, the recollection of that moment will be to him a source of pure, unfading happiness, nor will it shine least brightly in the evening of his days of noble usefulness.

"'The affection that exists between these two, the master and pupil, is as far removed from all ordinary care and regard, as the circumstances in which it has had its growth are apart from the common occurrences of life. He is occupied now in devising means of imparting to her higher knowledge, and of conveying to her some idea of the Great Creator of that universe in which, dark and silent and scentless though it be to her, she has such deep delight and glad enjoyment.

"'Ye who have eyes and see not, and have ears and hear not; ye who are as the hypocrites of sad countenances, and disfigure your faces that you may seem unto men to fast, learn healthy cheerfulness and mild contentment from the deaf and dumb and blind. Self-elected saints with gloomy brows, this sightless, earless, voiceless child may teach you lessons you may do well to follow. Let that poor hand of hers lie gently on your hearts; for there may be something in its healing touch akin to that of the Great Master whose precepts you misconstrue, whose lessons you pervert, of whose charity and sympathy with all the world not one among you in his daily practice knows as much as many of the worst among those fallen sinners to whom you are liberal in nothing but the preachment of perdition.

"'As I rose to quit the room, a pretty little child of one of the attendants came running in to greet its father. For the moment, a child with eyes among the sightless crowds, impressed me very painfully. Ah! how much brighter and more deeply blue, glowing and rich than it had been before, was the scene without, contrasting with the darkness of so many youthful lives within.'"

Having spoken at some length upon the education of the blind we will now conclude this subject with a few remarks concerning their achievements as given by the

Encyclopedia to which we have referred in a previous part of this chapter. Among the many instances of remarkable blind men, few are more worthy of record than the Rev. Dr. Willard, of Deerfield, Mass. Dr. Willard is now (1858) in his 83d year, and lost his sight, at least so far as ability to read was concerned, at the age of 43. He was already known favorably to the public by his writings on controversial, musical, and scientific subjects; but the commencement of his blindness seemed the beginning of a new era in his intellectual career. Within the forty years that have since intervened he has prepared and published: 1. A volume of hymns, composed by himself, each constructed with the purpose of making the rhetorical correspond with the musical rythm, a work of great labor; 2. A collection of hymns, from various authors; 3. A series of primary school books, which have enjoyed a large popularity; 4. "Principles of Rhetoric and Elocution;" 5. "Memorials of Daniel E. Parkhurst," one of his successors in the pastorate of the Congregational Church at Deerfield; 6. "The Grand Issue," an ethico-political pamphlet upon the relations of slavery; 7. "An Affectionate Remonstrance," with certain orthodox ministers and periodicals concerning the temper and style of religious controversy; 8. Several single sermons. Besides these, he has in manuscript an elaborate essay on phonography, to which subject he has devoted special attention for many years, and a work on the "Harmony of Musical and Poetical Expression."

During a considerable portion of the period in which he has been engaged upon these works he has had the care of a large parish. Dr. Willard is a man of very active habits, and performs with ease and readiness many of those arts for which we are accustomed to regard sight as indispensible. He gathers his own fruit, climbing the

trees readily, notwithstanding his age; prunes them carefully and judiciously; digs, lays out and plants his garden, selecting and sowing the seed without mistake; saws
and carries in his own wood, and seems almost unconscious of his privation. He has for the last twenty-five
years been completely blind, and for twelve years previous had only been able to distinguish large objects indistinctly; but even now, when closeted in his room, visions of the green fields and sunny slopes of the Connecti-
cut Valley appear to him as really as when he gazed upon
them with the eyes which for so long a period have admitted no light. He denies that this is imagination, but
regards it as an exhibition of one of the mysterious modes
in which the mind may hold communication with the
outer world without aid of the senses.

Notwithstanding his great age, there are no symptoms of failure in his intellectual powers. He has always
contended that the loss of memory and the vitiation of
the other mental faculties in the aged were the result of
mental inactivity; and as his own years rolled on, resolved to test his theory on his own case. In April, 1857,
at his own request, his memory was severely tested by a
friend. Of one hundred and ten passages of Scripture
selected at random from both the Old and New Testa-
ments read to him he gave, in nearly every instance, the
book, chapter and verse correctly at once. Of forty lines
taken from his "Hymns," he gave the hymn, verse and
line in nearly every instance. His memory was tested in
regard to the graduates of seven colleges, whose names
were called from the triennial catalogues, and he gave
readily the college and year of graduation of all persons
with whom he was acquainted, of all distinguished public and professional men, of all judges, presidents and pro-
fessors of colleges, members of the American Academy, &c.

A recent instance of a blind man pursuing his mental cultivation and practicing the duties of a profession with eminent success, is that of the blind minister, the Rev. Dr. Timothy Woodbridge, now living at Spencertown, N. Y. He was born at Stockbridge, Mass., in 1784. His mother was a daughter of the elder President Edwards, and one of his cousins was the renowned Aaron Burr.

During his second year in college he lost the sight of one eye by weakness and inflammation, caused by hard study and heightened by a severe cold. His remaining eye seemed at first strengthened in keenness and force by loss of the first; but before his college period was finished it became in like manner inflamed, and its sight was gradually extinguished. Mr. Woodbridge bore his misfortune with a philosophic and buoyant temper, received the commiseration of his associates with indifference or contempt, and at once accommodated his plans to the new circumstances in which he was placed. Selecting the profession of law, he formed large schemes of study, and with the aid of numerous young gentlemen who read to him, he not only mastered legal work, but studied thoroughly ancient and modern history, and went over the whole range of English classics from the age of Elizabeth.

He was cherishing political aspirations, and had gained some distinction as a political orator; when, in 1809, his attention being strongly drawn to the subject of religion, he experienced a religious change, and determined to devote himself to preaching the Gospel. He pursued theological studies at Andover, became acquainted with the most eminent ministers of the time, was admired as a preacher when he began the practice of his profession, and was for twenty-four years pastor at Green

River in the State of New York. It was his custom to have with him a young man who was skilled in reading and writing, and to whom he often dictated the heads of his sermons in order to stamp them the more deeply on his own memory. Yet he had so well trained himself that on Saturday evening he always had distinctly in mind not only the substance, but generally the form and language of the two or three sermons which he was to deliver the next day ; he was uniformly cheerful, and loved society ; and his recently published autobiography is interesting, not only for its genial and happy tone, but for its judicious reflections upon many notable men and works.

The Rev. William H. Milburn, another remarkable example of genius triumphing over apparently insuperable difficulties, was born in Philadelphia, September 26, 1823. He lost the sight of one eye irretrievably and of the other partially in early childhood. His own account of the amount of vision which remained to him, in an address at the publishers' festival in 1855, is as follows: "Time was when, after a fashion, I could read; but never with that flashing glance which instantly transfers a word, a line, a sentence, from the page to the mind. It was the perpetuation of the child's process, a letter at a time, always spelling, never reading truly. Thus, for more than twenty years, with the shade upon the brow, the hand upon the cheek, the finger beneath the eye to make an artificial pupil, with beaded sweat, joining with the hot tears trickling from the weak and paining organ, to blister upon the page, was my reading done."

Notwithstanding this serious disability in the way of obtaining an education, he was determined to accomplish it, and we find him, accordingly, at the age of 14, a clerk in a store in Illinois, endeavoring in his leisure moments to fit for college. He attained his purpose, passed through his collegiate course with honor, though at the cost of his health, which failed under the intense application which his imperfect vision rendered necessary.

At the age of 20 he entered the ministry in the Methodist Episcopal Church as an itinerant. In the course of twelve years' itinerancy he occupied fields in almost every part of the Union, and traveled over two hundred thousand miles in the performance of clerical duties, everywhere cordially received and welcomed not less for the amiability and modesty of his manners than for his extraordinary eloquence as a preacher and lecturer. He officiated as chaplain to Congress during two sessions, and with great acceptance. In 1853 he removed his family to New York city, where he has since resided, having left the circuit from the special inconvenience it entailed upon him, and since that time has preached as a supply to vacant churches, and followed the profession of a public lecturer, in which he has met with extraordinary success. In 1857 he published a volume of his lectures under the title of "Rifle, Axe, and Saddle-bags," which has had quite a large sale; the lectures were based on a solid substratum of facts, revealing high descriptive powers and a brilliant imagination.

Benjamin B. Bowen, of Massachusetts, was blind from infancy, and passed several years of his childhood as a fisher boy. He graduated in 1839 from the Perkins Institution for the Blind in Boston, and has, since then, been busily employed as a musician, lecturer and author. He published, in 1847, a duodecimo volume entitled the "Blind Man's Offering."

CHAPTER VI.

VACATION VISIT TO THE WEST—FINAL DEPARTURE FROM
THE INSTITUTION—I RESOLVED TO ENTER A SCHOOL OF
THE SEEING—REMARKS ON HILLSDALE COLLEGE AND MY
EXPERIENCE THERE.

After I had been at New York nearly four years I
concluded to make a tour through the West. There were
several friends whom I wished to visit on my way, but
my final destination was my aunt's family, with whom
I had lived while losing my eyesight, and who were at
this time residing in the State of Illinois. I was prompted to do this, partly because I wished to meet with those
whom I loved so much (for now that I was shut out from
the world around me my friends seemed much dearer to
me than before), and partly because my health was not
good enough to reap much benefit from the school. And
so, without feeling much regret at parting from the Institution, although I did not expect to return, I bade my
blind friends good-bye, and started with the intention of
making Mannsville my first destination.

Perhaps I should say in justice to the Institution,
that I received the kindest treatment during most of my
stay with them. The Superintendent, Mr. T. C. Cooper
(now deceased), was unusually kind to me during the last
two years, and the other officers of the Institution followed his example. Care was taken at every meal, that
my plate was supplied with something extra, not because
I was better than the other students, but because my
state of health justified this course; and I shall never

forget the kind regard the students manifested for me whenever an opportunity was afforded them. But notwithstanding all this, I felt that I should be more comfortable within the quiet homes of my friends, than I could expect to be within the walls of a public institution. I remained in the vicinity of Mannsville several weeks, and spent most of the time while there in selling bead-work manufactured by some lady graduates of our Institute who resided in New York. I found ready sale for these articles, partly on account of their being a curiosity and partly because the people wished to patronize those who were laboring under such disadvantages for their own support.

My next point of interest was South Valley, Cattaraugus county, N. Y., where lived an uncle whom I held in high esteem. My uncle's home was near the Alaghana Reservation, a tract of land reserved by the Six Nations, when they ceded a portion of their country to our government. Here I had an opportunity of becoming somewhat acquainted with the Indian character; for, although they were in general rather shy of us, yet one of their number proved to be an exception to the rule and made us frequent and prolonged visits. His dress consisted of pantaloons and shirt, fashioned like the Europeans; but, unlike them, he wore his shirt outside the other garments, which gave him rather a slouching appearance. He was very talkative, especially after partaking of a hearty dinner and several glasses of hard cider; then he was ready to tell us of the spirit land, to sing songs or to perform war dances, and would even go into a double shuffle whenever I played a lively tune for him on the violin. Of course I am not in favor of dancing as it is publicly managed, and would not be a fiddler, particularly a "blind fiddler," for any consideration whatever. But this old Indian danced in the day time, danced when he needed exercise, and stopped when he was weary—though on one occasion I determined to put his powers of endurance to the test, and so kept playing until my friends, fearing that he would become entirely exhausted, advised me to rest. As soon as the music ceased he threw himself into a chair, exclaiming almost breathlessly, "long song dat!"

A piece of information concerning the physical appearance of the natives gave me a little surprise. I was told that quite a number of them had blue eyes and light hair. Now I had learned from my geography, when a boy, that Indians had black eyes and dark hair, and I had never heard of an exception to this rule; but here it seems Dame Nature stepped out from her course and gave to the dusky savage a light complexion, blue eyes, and, in a few instances, golden tresses. But I will leave the solution of this mystery to others and resume my journey; for I have stayed in this place about seven weeks, which you will acknowledge is quite a *visitation*. The time, however, has been spent very pleasantly; for, besides the profitable reading we have enjoyed and the lively visit within doors, we have been almost daily to the river and have many times skated together over its frozen surface (for it is winter), and on one occasion we climbed nearly to the summit of a mountain that throws its giant shadows almost athwart the little valley where my uncle and his family reside.

After parting with my relatives and their aboriginal neighbors I proceeded on my way until I reached Hudson, Ohio, when a short ride brought me to the home of one of my father's sisters. This aunt was a young girl and lived at home with my grandmother during the time she had charge of me in my infancy, and, as might be expected, she and her family gave me a warm reception and provided me with every comfort while I remained with them. In fact she, like others of my friends, thought I ought to live with her as she was lonely and no one had any stronger claims upon me than herself.

My next stopping place was near Toledo, Ohio, where I was agreeably entertained by my friends with whom I lived at intervals during my sailor life, and, after spending a reasonable length of time with them, I journeyed on to Fremont, Indiana. My relative who had formerly resided in this place had removed, as I have before stated, to Illinois; but I found rich enjoyment in the company of my old neighbors, especially one whose daughter had been the companion of many school boy excursions. This family, like many others I have met, rallied me about some of my youthful blunders and experiences. They said, among other things, that when I wished Eunice to go with me, I would linger about the premises until she made her appearance. I was too bashful to enter the house. Of course I had not forgotten those things; nor had I forgotten the time when Eunice returned to me from her mother with the announcement that she could not be spared from home. This was the last invitation I gave her; for I was uncertain whether her mother prevented her from going, or whether she had framed this excuse to avoid my disapprobation. In justice, however, to Eunice, I will say that she has since informed me that she was vexed at her mother for not letting her go. But this, probably, is not the only time that my diffidence has deprived me of much enjoyment.

When I had completed my stay at Fremont I went directly to the home of my aunt with whom I was living at the time of my misfortune, and who was at this time residing near Seneca, La Salle county, Illinois. While at

her house, one of her sons, a namesake of mine, being of
an ambitious turn of mind, induced me to put forth some
efforts in the direction of obtaining a permanent home
and property for myself. He first proposed that I should
purchase a breaking team, as there was much unbroken
prairie in his vicinity, and he could manage the work for
me. This I accordingly did. The team consisted of two
yoke of oxen. The plan might have succeeded well had
not one of the oxen died before the breaking season was
entirely over. This threatened to be quite a disaster, for
cattle were very high at that time. My cousin, however,
sold the remaining ox for enough to buy a pair of young
steers which he raised free of charge for me. My aunt
also contributed by raising a steer to fill the dead one's
place, so that my loss was really a gain, as far as I was
individually concerned.

My cousin next proposed that I should establish a
broom manufactory, as I had devoted a portion of my
time while at the Institution for the Blind in learning
that trade. He promised to raise the broom corn and
build a shop for me on his premises if I would make my
home with him. I gladly acceded to the plan on condition that, before putting it into operation, I should return to New York and become better acquainted with the
business. On my return to New York I was cordially
received by the Superintendent of the Institution, who
wrote immediately to Albany for my re-appointment, as
the time of my first appointment had expired during my
stay in the West. He was not successful, however, in
his efforts in my behalf, for the reason that I was past
the age prescribed by the board of instruction for the admission of pupils into the school, and my case was not
considered an exception to the rule. But this disappointment did not defeat my purpose; for while waiting for

returns from Albany, I became slightly acquainted with the overseer of the broom shop, a young man partially blind, and our acquaintanceship resulted in a proposal on his part to accompany me into the country and teach me the broom trade, providing I would share equally with him the proceeds of our labor. As this was a better opportunity than the Institution could have afforded me, I readily accepted it; and, as soon as matters could be arranged for the young man's departure, we set out for Mannsville *en route* for Seneca, Illinois. John (as my new friend was generally called) was an Englishman by birth, and, judging by his manner and the letters he received while we were together, was of very respectable parentage. When a little more than twenty years of age he bade adieu to his nation, England, to seek his fortune in the new world, a world at that time peopled with entire strangers to him. Soon after his arrival in this country he engaged with a partner to work in an iron mine a few miles from New York city. This business was yielding him a fair income when it was suddenly cut short by the unexpected explosion of a blast which he was superintending. This accident resulted in the loss of all the fingers of his right hand with the exception of his thumb, and also the entire loss of his sight. His life would probably have been sacrificed had it not been for a heavy hat which he wore at the time, the hat itself being blown into a thousand fragments. Immediately after this accident he was taken to the city and placed in a hospital where he was kindly attended until his wounds were healed and partial sight restored in one of his eyes. The sight he received, however, was barely sufficient to enable him to discern large objects at a short distance and decipher coarse reading matter when the print was within a few inches of his face. In this condition he offered himself as a student to the Institution for the Blind and was finally accepted, although his foreign birth made it difficult for him to obtain this object. Soon after his admission into the Institution he requested permission to learn the broom trade; but here a new difficulty assailed him. The shop was thronged with journeymen and applicants for the business, and the man who had it in charge, with others, declared that no man whose hand was so badly deformed could make brooms; but, notwithstanding, they were obliged to admit him into their ranks, and John, with a spirit of determination that would have done honor to Napoleon himself, labored incessantly and with so much success that, in a few months, he was acknowledged the best workman among the students, and was soon after raised to the position of overseer, in which capacity he was acting at the time of our meeting.

It was, of course, a matter of surprise, both to the people of the Institution and my friends at home, that one so well qualified for business, and holding so good a situation, should go with one who was almost an entire stranger to him; but I think he never regretted this course, although we were not as successful financially as we could have wished. John was about five feet six inches in height, strongly built, and rather prepossessing in appearance, although he was somewhat disfigured by his misfortune. He had an active mind, a generous disposition, and great conversational abilities, although he rarely conversed with any except his most intimate friends. He was at that time—and for aught I know, is yet—unmarried.

Soon after our arrival at Mannsville we concluded to spend a few months in that vicinity, as my cousin in Illinois was not quite prepared to receive us; and to make the time pass pleasantly we visited among my friends and relatives, and engaged them to raise corn for us to manufacture.

As broom material at that time was nearly as dear as when made up, we concluded not to work at our trade until our own corn should be ready for use. Meantime we determined not to be idle, and we purchased some maps, and, each with a small bundle under his arm, we started out, hand in hand, to dispose of them. In this operation we succeeded very well, as it was in time of the war, when maps of our country were in greater demand than they otherwise would have been. We also obtained some pleasure as well as profit from our employment, and occasionally an incident took place which greatly amused us; for instance, while stopping at the house of a friend in whose vicinity we were acquainted, we were in the habit of taking a morning walk, partly for pastime, and partly for the benefit the exercise afforded us. In a short time after our coming we were surprised to learn that our presence had created considerable excitement among the inhabitants for some distance around. It had been reported that two suspicious looking strangers, probably "rebel spies," were lurking in the neighborhood. They were even patroling the country in the daytime; but they invariably returned before evening to pass the night in the woods. On some occasions they were observed to be walking at a rapid pace at some distance from the rendezvous, but they took no notice of anybody by the roadside, although the people had frequently run out to their gates to attract their attention. Poor souls! If they had known that the defective sight of one eye guided us both, they would not have found fault with us for not staring at them; and if they had followed us along our woodland path to the comfortable residence of our friend, they would have known that we were enjoying as comfortable lodgings as themselves. But these people, like many others at that time, were so much excited by the rebellion, that they looked with suspicion and dread upon nearly all who came among them.

Soon after this another event transpired which furnished more amusement for those who witnessed it than to myself. We were visiting at the house of a friend where a little old lady was stopping at the same time. Being desirous of playing with the children, I caught hold, as I supposed, of a young girl who was standing near me, and drew her on my lap. But John, who was sitting by my side, was able to see sooner than I could feel my mistake, and so hurriedly exclaimed, "Harvey, you have got the grandmother!" Upon this I relaxed my hold, and the old lady scampered off as soon as she could recover her feet, as much frightened as myself, though not displeased with me; she had too much sense to take umbrage at an innocent blunder.

Another advantage I received from traveling was the information I received from John, which he would not otherwise have given me; for, although he was a man of taciturnity when in company, and would sit for hours without speaking a word except to answer in monosyllables the questions put to him, yet when we were by ourselves he would converse so freely and eloquently that I thought him one of the wisest men I had ever known, and felt certain that he must have spent his life in profound study and meditation. But since then, on a little reflection, I have concluded that he obtained much of his knowledge from the conversation of others. Much more is gained by listening than by talking continually, as many do as long at they can obtain a hearing. Among other things which John related to me of his former life, he mentioned his having a cow while in England—the best cow, he said, he had ever known. Her cream would bear up a plate, and she produced three pounds of butter a day. This seemed to be a marvelous story, but John was in one of his most serious moods, and I, therefore, could not question its truthfulness. In fact, I had so much confidence in his integrity and sagacity, that had he told me his cow's cream would hold up an iron wedge, and her butter supply a whole neighborhood, I should have considered it almost infidelity to doubt a word of the assertion.

When autumn came with its golden harvests, it brought to John and myself many parcels of fine broom corn which we readily converted into substantial brooms and brushes, receiving as a recompense a portion of the manufactured articles, or a stipulated sum of money, according to the option of our patrons. Our stores brought the highest market price, and in a few months after commencing our labors, we manufactured and disposed of all the corn that had been raised for us. When spring opened we set out, according to arrangement, for Illinois, and arrived at our destination in time to encourage my cousin and others to put in a good quantity of seed. We also hired several acres of newly broken ground, and planted it for ourselves. This kind of sward needs no tilling for the first crop, except to chop in the seed, and this John and I could do nearly as well as others, his sight being sufficient to enable him to follow the furrows, while I could be guided by the sound of his movements. So, arming ourselves each with an axe and a pocket of seed, we commenced our task, and pursued it diligently until it was done, being assured, meanwhile, that if the rows were crooked, they would be longer than straight ones, and consequently would yield more corn!

When planting was over, John, being able to perform some kinds of farm work to advantage, hired to my cousin until our crop should come in, while I busied myself with listening to reading, and visiting my friends and neighbors. In this way we passed the time pleasantly until our corn was ready to harvest, when we went to work with all the help we could command, which was barely sufficient for the purpose, to gather it in. The crop, however, was very well secured, considering the circumstances, and as soon as it was cured and prepared for use by ridding it of its seed, we began to manufacture it with a zeal fully commensurate with our ability, which, so far as John was concerned, was not inconsiderable. I mention the fact of my incompetency because it was a great discomfort to me. My lack of strength, of practice and of ingenuity gave me a continual sense of my inferiority, though John never uttered a word of complaint. On the other hand, he took everything patiently, and sent me out to sell the brooms, to purchase the twine and handles and do similar work, which he seemed to think me better qualified for than himself.

How long I might have continued in this employment had it been conducive to my health, I cannot tell—probably for a life-time, however; for it was yielding me a fair income, and I was much delighted with the prospect of having a steady home—but I was finally forced to the conclusion that the broom-corn dust was injuring me, and would eventually undermine my health. I should, notwithstanding this, have continued longer at the business, had it not been for a fancy I had taken for public speaking; and, knowing that I was not qualified for this pursuit, and could not obtain the required advantages while staying in the country, I was obliged to give up entirely my interest in the broom trade, in order to carry out my plans. This arrangement was not wholly original with me; it had been suggested by my friends that I was capa-

ble of preaching the Gospel, and ought to improve my
gift. As for myself, I was not inclined to this view; for,
although I was deeply interested in the cause of Chris-
tianity, I could not bear to bring upon myself the responsibility which this calling would incur, but was satisfied
with the idea of lecturing upon such popular subjects as
I could make available. Accordingly, after spending the
winter and a portion of the following spring as agreeably
as the circumstances could possibly admit, I settled up
my affairs with John and my relatives, and set out with
the hope of finding some institution of learning where I
could obtain reading from the students and could listen
to their recitations and other exercises.

My first stopping place was at Chicago, where I obtained a guide who conducted me to the Theological Seminary of that city. On reaching our destination, I presented to the faculty of the institution a letter of recom-
mendation from a minister of their acquaintance. After
reading the letter and listening attentively to my story,
they told me kindly that they did not see how I could be
benefitted by coming among them; one of their number
remarking at the same time, that "if he were blind, he
should cease all efforts in his own behalf; for it was evident that a blind person could do nothing to advantage."
They did not, however, banish all hope from my mind;
but promised to do all they could if I should, after more
reflection, conclude to return. Thanking them for their
kindness I bade them adieu with an inward determination not to visit them again, but to seek my fortune else-
where.

I had come to Chicago under the impression that
my letter of introduction would gain for me all the privileges of the Seminary that I could appropriate; and the
disappointment bore down more heavily, because I had

no passport to another institution, except what I might say in my own behalf. But I had severed entirely my business relations with John and my cousin, and there was nothing left me now but to follow this glimmer of hope, until it should lead me to a brighter sphere, or should dissipate itself in the gloom which hovered around. Soon after leaving Chicago I learned that there was a college of high repute at Hillsdale, Michigan, and thither I bent my steps, or rather "groped my way;" for it must be acknowledged that a blind man, traveling among strangers, cannot discern his path very clearly nor very far in advance of him. Although my progress was slow, I went directly to an "open sesame," as though I had possessed the best of sight, and was afterward convinced that my disappointment at Chicago, like many others I have suffered, was all for the best.

Immediately after my arrival at Hillsdale I found a fine old German gentleman, to whose family I had been conducted, who took me to his house to stay with him over the Sabbath; and this favor he repeated as often as he could find the opportunity during the whole of my stay in this place. On the first of the following week I called upon Dr. Fairfield, the President of the college, who received me kindly and informed me that I was welcome to all the instruction I could obtain. He also took pains to introduce me to the senior professor and other members of the faculty, and did all in his power to make me feel at home in my new situation. The President, like most of our great men, had risen to his position mainly through his own efforts, and was, therefore, well prepared to sympathize with those who were endeavoring to help themselves. He had also been among the first and most prominent in founding the institution, and, consequently, had a right to place me under its patronage.

It has sometimes been inferred, from what has been said concerning my course at Hillsdale, that this is a school for the blind; but this is not the case. I am the only one of my class who has been a student there (1872), and I was to gain my information by having the students read their lessons to me, and by listening to recitations and oral exercises.

As some account of Hillsdale College may be of interest to those who wish to educate themselves in one of the first institutions of our land, I will here insert an article which has been clipped from a recent number of the *Michigan Land Journal:*

"Hillsdale, the seat of Hillsdale College, is a flourishing city in Southern Michigan. By means of the Lake Shore & Michigan Southern, and the Detroit, Hillsdale & Indiana Railroads, which pass through it, communication is had with all parts of the country. By these routes it is distant one hundred and eighty miles east of Chicago, sixty west of Toledo, and eighty southwest of Detroit.

"The College building is a fine structure two hundred and sixty-two feet in length, and four stories high exclusive of the basement. The grounds surrounding it are ample and well laid out. It is sufficiently near to the business part of the city to accommodate students in all matters which may legitimately call them there, and yet is so far removed as to secure that quiet which is essential to the successful prosecution of study.

"Chartered February 9th, 1855, it was opened for the admission of students November 7th of the same year. Since that time it has sent out 220 graduates and had in attendance about 3,500 under-graduates. It has three regular courses of study, Classical, Scientific and Ladies', besides Theological, Commercial, Music and Art Departments.

"According to the last catalogue, the Seniors in the several departments number 30; Juniors, 44; Sophomores, 50; Freshmen, 81; Classical Preparatory, 28; General Preparatory, 224; other departments, 201; making a total for the year's attendance of 658, representing sixteen States, the District of Columbia and the Canadas. The graduates at the last commencement numbered 29.

"The institution is under the control of 35 Trustees, two-thirds of whom are required by the constitution to be members of the Frewill Baptist denomination. All prudential matters are entrusted to a committee of nine local members, except during annual and special meetings of the Board of Trustees.

"The College has from the first been open to all without distinction of sex or color. There are five well-sustained Literary Societies, three among the gentlemen and two among the ladies. They contribute much to the culture of their members, and afford many instructive and interesting occasions for others. Five beautiful and well-furnished halls are under their control, some of them containing large libraries and fine collections of natural history.

"All students have free use of the College Library, which contains more than 3,000 volumes. The expenses are always low, the cost of instruction not exceeding $5 per annum, except in the Commercial, Art and Music departments.

"To all members of the graduating class of the Classical department, the Trustees grant diplomas conferring the degree of Bachelor of Arts, and to those of the Scientific department and Ladies' course the degree of Bachelor of Science.

"The Faculty of Instruction is composed of thirteen members, as follows:

" Rev. Daniel M. Graham, D. D., President.

" Rev. Ransom Dunn, A. M., Professor of Biblical Theology.

" Rev. Spencer J. Fowler, A. M , Professor of Mathematics and Natural Philosophy.

" George McMillan, A. M., Professor of Greek and Latin Languages.

" Hiram Collier, A. M., Professor of Natural Science.

" F. Wayland Dunn, A. M., Professor of Rhetoric and Belles Lettres.

" Miss H. Laura Rowe, A. M., Principal of Ladies' Department.

" A. C. Rideout, Principal Commercial Department and Professor of Commercial Law.

" W. A. Drake, Assistant Principal and Instructor in Commercial Arithmetic and Penmanship.

" George B. Gardner, Instructor in Painting and Drawing.

" M. W. Chase, Instructor in Instrumental and Vocal Music.

" Mrs. Olive C. Chase, Instructor in Culture of the Voice.

" Miss Jennie de la Montagnie, Teacher of French.

" L. P. Reynolds, Secretary and Treasurer.

" Hillsdale College occupies the honorable position of being next in point of numbers and thoroughness of instruction to the State University, and at present and prospectively gives promise of a grand position in the future."

After I had become acquainted with the students, and they had learned my object in coming, I found no difficulty in obtaining all the reading I needed, and their interest in my welfare was more apparent when I began to take an active part in the recitations. I also found much enjoyment and profit in attending the literary societies of the college. Two of these, the Theological and Amphyction, invited me to join them, which I did, although it was not without a struggle that I made up my mind to appear before a college audience. One of these societies held its first anniversary after my initiation, and I was chosen as one of the speakers for the occasion. My exercise was entitled "A Sermon on Tobacco," which, for the sake of variety, I will introduce here, being indebted for its preservation to a health journal, which published it a few days after this event:

TEXT.—"Tobacco is an evil weed," &c.

In discussing the subject of tobacco, we do not labor under the embarrassment which generally accompanies the reproval of other abnormal habits; for the devotees of this giant evil seldom advocate its claims, but, on the other hand, strongly denounce the system as being injurious in its very nature, admonishing those around them to beware of the course they themselves have so unwittingly followed. True, at times, when chided by those as deeply enthralled as themselves, they will, by a keen retort, silence their accusers. A circumstance of this kind took place not long since in one of our Western States. A tobacco user on being reproved by an inveterate tea drinker, asked in return why she did not give up her tea. The lady replied that the water in that vicinity was so impure that it needed tea to render it palatable. "Very well," said he, "your case is similar to mine, for the atmosphere of this country is so impure that it must be cleansed by tobacco smoke before it is fit for respiration."

Of course we do not deem this practice [the crying sin of the age, but only one of the many forms of intemperance which degrade humanity and demand a warning voice from every philanthropic member of society. Our

text is not contained verbatim in the Holy Scriptures, for
when they were written, the evil did not exist; but if it
be an evil, it is all the more important that its character
should be exhibited, and its effects made known to all
whom it may concern. Our subject is embodied in the
following stanza:

"Tobacco is an evil weed,
    And from the Devil did proceed;
It picks the pockets, burns the clothes,
    And makes a chimney of the nose."

And, *first,* "It is an evil weed."

It is classified with hen bane, thorn apple, deadly
nightshade, and other poisonous weeds; being three times
more potent than opium in the same form. One drop of
the distilled oil, placed on the tongue of the stoutest dog,
produces instant death. The cat, which is said to have
nine lives, yields them up in less than three minutes after
the application of the second drop. An eminent writer
declares that if a man were to dip both of his hands into
this oil, with a skillful surgeon by his side, they could
not be amputated in time to save his life. As an article
of food it sustains but two species of the animal kingdom: the loathsome tobacco worm, at the sight of which
humanity recoils with disgust, and the rock goat of
Africa, whose stench is so insufferable that no other animal can approach it. Man and other animals which
esteem it a luxury, have learned to do so at the expense
of nausea and nervous prostration, or received the appe-
tite from intemperate predecessors. If, as has been
claimed, it has medicinal properties, it should be applied
like other remedies, and its use abandoned when the result is attained; but if the cure is not speedily performed
it should be condemned as other noxious quackeries.

Second, "And from the Devil did proceed."

It has ever been the object of him who introduced sin into the world, and thereby hurled the firebrand of destruction into the bosom of the human family, to deteriorate the physical and moral condition of those subjected to his influence. This work is successfully accomplished by the agency of tobacco.

It deranges the physical system. Nature, as an auxiliary in the work of alimentation, has prepared three sets of glands which moisten the mouth, assist the taste, and further aid in the work of digestion. When anything is taken into the mouth, these glands pour forth a copious supply of their fluids till the substance is removed, or their resources are exhausted. The use of tobacco not only robs alimentation of this essential assistant, but its waste renders the membrane so febrile that stimulating beverages seem requisite to supply the deficiency. Thus, other passions are aroused, which it requires continued efforts to restrain. The work of the Christian is to overcome and hold in subjection the propensities of our animal nature; hence, whatever tends to strengthen them at the expense of the moral powers, is so far a sin. The legitimate use of all our appetites and passions is not only in strict accordance with divine will, but essential to our well being and happiness. But every violation of the physical law is an aggression upon the moral domain, and effects a corresponding influence upon the spiritual character of the transgressors. Hence the command, "Be ye temperate in all things," and, to your knowledge add temperance. In reference to this matter, says Dr. Clarke: "Were I to present a sacrifice to the Devil, I would stuff a pig with tobacco, and lay it upon the altar."

Third, "It picks the pockets, burns the clothes."

It is claimed that the victimized subjects of tobacco

are a fine, generous set of people, willing to divide the last quid with a suffering friend. We admit this to be true, and our love for them prompts us to make an effort to convert them from the error of their ways; and when we take a pecuniary view of the matter, and estimate the enormous sum of money expended in a worse than useless cause, their benevolence, we trust, will lead them to appropriate their means in another direction. In this country alone, the annual expenditure is not less than forty millions of dollars. One-fifth of the amount is spent by church-going people. Consider for a moment the blessing their means would be to the world. Think of the improvement that could be made in our canals, our harbors, our railroads, and other public works. How the poor might be relieved, the gospel dispensed, and the happy change of circumstances which would result. And all this without taking into account the filthiness of the habit, and its consequent destruction of clothing, furniture and other property.

God is able to convert the world by miracle, or to send money from Heaven for its accomplishment, but he has committed the charge to men and angels. Suppose one of the angelic beings should visit the earth with a proclamation, and you should discover in his mouth an immense quid of tobacco, and see him pour forth a deluge of the golden juice upon everything which came in his way. You would declare at once that he was an emissary from his satanic majesty, and had better save his effusions to moisten the atmosphere in his own habitation.

Fourth, "And makes a chimney of the nose."

The all wise and benevolent Author of the Universe has made nothing in vain, but in every department of creation we behold blended in harmonious perfection, beauty and adaptation of purpose. In no organ do we find these qualities more rarely displayed than in the human nose. Standing in conspicuous relationship to the other features, it not only gives expression to the countenance, but with its keen perceptions admonishes its possessor against the encroachment of injurious odors. But the use of tobacco perverts its function, and destroys its relish for the perfumes of nature, and this abuse without the shadow of a reason. Addressing a venerable snuffer, we said, "Had nature designed this indulgence, your nose would have been inverted." She mildly answered:

"The pinch of snuff hath magic power
To soften many a gloomy hour;
For though the world may use me rough,
I'll smile, and take my pinch of snuff."

This kind of pleasure is too dearly bought, for every gratification at the expense of nature's laws is followed by suffering correspondingly great.

Then if the use of tobacco is inimical to our physical, moral and spiritual well-being, if it is a needless expenditure of means which should be otherwise appropriated, and creates necessities before unknown, why not abandon it at once? Why persist in a course detrimental to our own happiness and that of others? And, oh! if it be ours when done with the toils of earth, to soar away to the mansions of the blest, could we, if permitted, unblushingly mar the beauties of the place with effusions of the weed? Or, think you angelic beings with golden spittoons will be detailed to transport the rich production to some stygian pool without the city? Depend upon it, no such provision will be made. Every intemperate habit must be overcome ere we can stand without spot or wrinkle before the judgment seat of the Omniscient.

Christian brethren, upon you devolves the duty of reproving iniquity wherever it may be found; and as you go forth exposing the moral condition of the people, remember, the physical equally claims your attention. In fine, follow the example of the apostle. Reason to them of righteousness, temperance and judgment to come.

When I had been in the college about two years, I was informed by my classmates, that they wished me to finish the course with them; and soon afterward President Fairfield told me that if I would study vigorously through the following year, he would, at the end of that period, graduate me, if the other members of the faculty were agreed in the matter. This I accordingly did, and at the time specified (June, 1868,) received the degree of Bachelor of Science, the President remarking on the occasion, that "although my diploma was partly honorary, in consequence of there being some branches which I could not pursue to advantage, if they (the public) knew of my standing, they would not think that it was unworthily bestowed." Thus ended my student life at Hillsdale, but not my stay in that place, for I have since spent many happy hours in and about the college, and have still the satisfaction of knowing that I shall be welcome there whenever I choose to return.

CHAPTER VII.

CONCLUSION.

Having sketched a few of the principal incidents of my life, and described briefly two institutions of learning from which I have obtained a portion of the little knowledge I possess, I will ask you, my friends, to tarry but a little longer while I shall say a few words concerning my vocation. I might with propriety dispense with this were it not for the consideration that some will be at a loss to know whether I have made any application of the advantages I have received, or whether the labors of my instructors have been entirely misplaced.

It is probable that most of those who are acquainted with my history will be disappointed in not finding in their memoirs some items which they judge worthy of insertion. But permit me to say, by way of apology, that I have written hastily and have determined to avoid, if possible, the opprobrium of wearying my readers with unnecessary details; in fact, whenever I attempt to write I am reminded of that time-honored maxim, " Brevity is the soul of wit," and this is often enforced by the recollection of a similar passage from the pen of an American critic, who declares that the preacher who cannot "strike ile" in twenty minutes must be using the wrong tool or boring in the wrong place. Still, on reflection, I think I might have been a little more explicit without serious injury to anyone, and most readers would have been better pleased thereby. For instance, when I recorded a narrow escape from drowning, I could have mentioned in that connection several similar escapes from an untimely end, which seemed equally providential. Again, I have spoken of the kindness of President Fairfield, and I will here add, for it is not too late to acknowledge this debt of gratitude, that his example was well followed by the people of the college and others whose acquaintance I made during my stay. My tuition, my room rent, and even my diploma were given me gratuitously, the treasurer replying to my urgent request that he should accept remuneration, that he would sooner pay the indebtedness himself than have it said that the college charged me for anything I received. Whenever I wished to go anywhere there was some one ready to accompany me until I was sufficiently acquainted with the premises and the neighboring streets to go readily by myself. I also received many presents while there. The donors knowing that I felt delicate about receiving assistance, would contrive to present their gifts in a manner which would have been acceptable to the most fastidious.

Once more—for now that I am nearing the end of my story I am getting somewhat over my hurry; in fact, I am beginning to learn that there is not much good accomplished by doing things in haste. How often it happens that we start for the railroad depot with our satchels half packed and arrive there in a state of perspiration to find that we are many minutes in advance of the time, and the train is as many minutes behind. Then, too, we frequently hurry off to church and have for our pains the pleasure of waiting until we are weary for the service to commence. The first of these evils we cannot well avoid; for sometimes we shall find that our watches agree with the railroad chronometers and the train will be sometimes on time. But for the other, I have adopted a plan which works to a charm—I go to church fifteen minutes late. But what I was going to say was simply a few words in regard to my health. Perhaps you will think that I have said enough about this matter already; and so I have if my intention is to keep up the dismal strain I have been harping on in the preceding pages. I am aware of the fact that it is not in good taste to be constantly parading our ills before others. Those who practice this, as many do for the sake of obtaining the sympathy of their weary listeners, ought to know that they are more likely to excite their disgust. If good can be accomplished or relief can be obtained in this way, it is all right; otherwise it is selfish and unbecoming.

As sickness was partly the occasion of my loss of sight, and as I was obliged for the same reason to change my employment, I thought it necessary to allude to it by way of explanation, and now, as my health is greatly improved, so much so that I live entirely free from pain and am as vigorous as my in-door life will allow, I wish to say a few words in regard to the means adopted for my recovery, that others may be benefitted thereby. And first, let me remark that this better state of things was not brought about by the use of patent nostrums nor similar specifics; for during many years of my sickness I took medicine enough to kill a horse or any other animal unless it be a donkey, (I make this exception, not knowing but that there is an analogy in our nature and, consequently, a similarity of endurance), and grew no better until I had abandoned these and begun to study and practice rules of health. I have noticed that whatever else the skillful physician prescribes, he always insists that his patients shall adopt a strict regimen of diet and pay particular attention to ventilation, cleanliness, rest, exercise, etc. In fact some of the most prominent in this profession have declared that drugs cannot benefit mankind in any way. But notwithstanding these principles are constantly advocated by honest physicians and others, it is difficult to make people believe that their habits of life have anything to do with their condition of health, and when obliged by sickness to desist from their unphysiological course until they have become well again, they always attribute their recovery to some panacea they have taken or to the miraculous interposition of Divine Providence. Now I do not intend to disparage in any way the power and goodness of Divine Providence nor His special love for our race; for certainly the Great Being who created us can, if He chooses, restore us when we are sick or keep us in permanent youth and vigor; and if the tiny sparrows are subjects of His zealous care, how much more so are we who are made after His own image and for whom He sacrificed His only begotten Son. But notwithstanding this, it is evident from what we have learned from His dealings with mankind that He does not, as a general thing, manifest His miraculous power in the preservation of life and health. This, I think, is farther manifested from His command to preserve our own lives and the lives of others, and His denunciations against the suicide and the murderer, declaring that He will destroy him who destroys his own body which He designates as a temple of the Holy Spirit, and threatening to bar from the Kingdom of Heaven the one who shall take the life of another. In fact God is not only a creator, but a ruler as well. The rolling spheres, as they traverse with unvarying precision the endless cycles which He has assigned them, proclaim Him Lord of all; and the smallest atom that is borne upon the wings of the evening zephyr bears equal testimony to His sovereign sway. All animated nature likewise acknowledges the same allegiance to His supreme will. Every variety of its production lives, grows, decays and dies in strict accordance with the laws of its organism. And having established these laws of nature it is, of course, essential to His honor that they meet the ends for which they were designed. And, in order to effect this purpose, He has established rewards and punishments as a consequence of their obedience or their transgression. These laws being adapted in their nature to the peculiarities of their subject, their consequences are also varied and peculiar in their operation; for instance, a ship floats because her hull displaces an amount of matter equal to her weight; and so long as this law of gravitation is observed, she will ride in safety, although her passengers and crew be pirates and debauchees. If, on the other hand, in consequence of bad management, this physical law be broken so that the vessel fill with water, it will go to the bottom, even if all on board be missionaries and temperance people. So in the organic sphere, if a man is born of healthy parents and he himself lives in accordance with the laws of his being, he will enjoy health and long life. While, on the other hand, if he or his parents violate these laws, he will suffer the consequences, which are disease and untimely death, and this without special reference to moral or spiritual character.

From these considerations it is evident that our health depends mainly upon our own voluntary action with reference to the laws of our being; and, as many of our habits of life are founded in ignorance of these laws, they are more likely to be in opposition to them than otherwise. Proceeding on this hypothesis I have studied the writings of those who have devoted their attention to this subject, and adopted such of their suggestions as I deemed practical and consistent. Among the works which I have read on this subject, those of Saxe, of Combe, and of Lewis, I think, contain the most reliable

information.   I would also recommend a periodical
which is now being published at Battle Creek, Michigan,
entitled the *Health Reformer*.

As a result of my improved condition of health I
enjoy a much happier state of mind; in fact, I am,
at times, almost as cheerful as when in possession of
sight, though it is evident from my general demeanor and
expression that my sorrows have traced themselves so
deeply upon me that they cannot be entirely obliterated.
Still I am learning daily to bear my misfortune with more
fortitude and submission; for I think I discover that in
this, as well as in most other afflictions, there is comparative recompense.   For instance, the tender care bestowed upon me by my friends whenever I am with them,
and the interest manifested for my welfare by strangers
wherever I go, have had a tendency to develop my better
nature and make me more charitable toward others.
Then, too, my many narrow escapes from imminent danger while traveling by myself have caused me to feel
more deeply my dependence upon the guiding hand of
the Supreme, and given me a more exalted sense of his
loving kindness and special care for those who cannot
care for themselves, inducing, thereby, a spirit of devotion
and trust.   Others, too, have been benefitted indirectly by
my affliction, as they often declare that my cheerfulness under my great affliction is a reproof to them whenever they
are inclined to complain of their trifling mishaps.   Another source of happiness is derived from my occupation ;
for now that I am able, through the patronage of a sympathizing public, to sustain myself honorably in society (a
matter which must be gratifying to any who possess in the
slightest degree the noble spirit of self-maintenance), I am
much more reconciled to my condition than I could possibly be were I a subject of charity or even in the posses-

sion of wealth with no means of employing my time to advantage.

And this reminds me of my promise to speak of my vocation, which I will proceed at once to do with as much brevity as the circumstances will admit. My motive in going to Hillsdale, as before stated, was to fit myself for the lecture field, and, to accomplish this purpose, I devoted my attention principally to those branches which would assist me in this direction, either as disciplinary or as themes for discourse. Among the latter I selected the science of Physiology as being the most available at that time, and finally arranged two lectures on that subject which I delivered, occasionally, in the vicinity of Hillsdale during the remainder of my stay. Since leaving the college I have spoken on the following topics: *What a Blind Man Saw in College, How the Blind See, What a Blind Man Saw Among the Stars*, and *Temperance.* The last of these, though somewhat trite, is acceptable in most places, and I am inclined to make it my favorite theme, as I think much good can be accomplished thereby, especially in restraining the youth from becoming dissipated in their daily habits.

Through the assistance of the college people and other influential friends, I have lectured with good success in many of the cities and villages of the Northwest, and also in northern New York, the best churches in these places opening their doors freely for this purpose and taking for my benefit a contribution or an admittance fee. Several railroad companies have also assisted me in my labors by granting me a free pass over their roads, and newspaper editors have advertised me free of charge, repeating their favor whenever I visited their localities.

Although I have been well received by the intelligent and sympathetic wherever I have been, yet I am aware of the fact that eye-sight is essential to the highest success in oratory. It needs the eye as well as the voice to rivet the attention and thrill the soul of him who listens. Still the deep sympathy created in the minds of the audience for one who has lost his vision compensates, in a great measure, for the embarrassment it occasions. And if the blind speaker is convinced that his efforts are appreciated, there is no reason why he should not persevere and do all in his power to benefit those who come within his sphere of action.

But the time has come for me to finish my story, and as I have dictated this sketch without any expectation of distinguishing myself for beauty of style or profundity of thought, I shall not attempt to startle any one in the conclusion, but will say to you, my friends, as I have often said when parting from your generous firesides, Good-bye! It may be we shall meet again.

POEMS.

POEMS.

THE RECONCILIATION.

By her little cottage door,
    'Neath a shady maple tree,
Sat a woman blind and poor,
    Pondering o'er her destiny.

Thinking of the wondrous change,
    Which the hand of Time had wrought;
Placing her beyond the range
    Of the blessings light had brought.

Sad she seems, and pale, and worn;
    And around her furrowed brow,
Where once clustered raven curls,
    Silver tresses glisten now.

And her form, so stiff and bent,
    Once was firm, erect and strong;
And her voice, now dissonant,
    Then rang out in merry song.

Now, the heart oppressed with care,
    Bleeding, comfortless and rent,
Once was free as mountain air—
    Saw no cause for discontent.

Where once played the merry feet
    Of the children she had borne,
Silence reigned, or others came;
    Now their absence she must mourn.

And the husband of her youth,
    In whose love she hoped to dwell,
Long ago had left her side,
    Driven to a maniac's cell.

Oh the bitterness and hate
    That within her bosom dwelt,
Toward the God who gave her birth,
    And for her no pity felt!

Leaving her in darkness there,
    Deep and hopeless as the tomb,
Closing every avenue
    Where the light of hope could come.

Just as if she were a *thing*
    He had made, and needed not,
To upbuild creation with,
    And had flung aside, forgot.

Thus she sat, from day to day,
    Now in madness, now in grief;
Dark, bewildered, and alone,
    Dreaming never of relief.

When there broke upon her soul
    Light celestial from above,
Chasing darkness far away,
    Filling it with beams of love.

Then a voice of heav'nly tone,
  Whispered softly in her ear:
"Those who put their trust in God,
  Have no need or cause for fear.

"He who tempers to shorn lambs
  All the cold and wintry blasts,
Feels for those His image bear,
  And protection round them casts;

"And, according to thy need,
  Shall thy strength and wisdom be;
And if faithful to the end,
  Thou at last shall reign with me.

And within that blissful place
  Where shall dwell no woe nor pain,
Thou shalt have thy sight restored,
  And behold thy friends again.

"And the glories of that sphere
  Shall the brighter seem to thee,
For the darkness thou hast seen,
  And thy untold misery.

"Little dost thou know, my child,
  What thy future might have been,
Had thy path been strewn with flowers.
  With no thorns to intervene.

"Others, too, by seeing thee
  Humbled 'neath this chastisement,
Will appreciate their lot,
  And be free from discontent."

9

Then the vision passed away ;
    But before it took its flight,
There were planted in her heart
    Fountains of pure love and light.

Still she lives, but not to mourn
    O'er her trials, though severe,
But rejoices in the hope
    That her promised rest is near.

TO COUSIN MARY.

Mary, my thoughts are with thee still,
    Where'er thou mayest be ;
Thou art, as thy name signifies,
    A star above the sea.

A star like that which God has set
    Within the northern skies,
That guides the mariner's frail bark,
    The bondsman when he flies.

And so with me while on life's sea,
    Mid storms and tempests' roar,
And threat'ning billows dashing high
    Against the rock-bound shore.

I'll trust in thee, my dearest friend—
    Thou art my guiding star ;
No other can eclipse thy light,
    No cloud thy beauty mar.

THE SEQUEL.

My star has set ; its trembling rays
    No more illume my lonely path ;
Ah, tell me, Thou who reignest above,
    Why was it subject to thy wrath?

Why was a thing that Thou hast made
    So pure and beautiful and just,
Struck from its firmament of love,
    And, reeling, sent to crumbling dust?

A whispering answer from the skies
    Comes like a zephyr o'er the sea ;
To cool my brow and aching breast,
    And fill my soul with ecstasy.

It says, "Thy star is set, 'tis true,
    And hid within the cold damp earth,
But in that realm beyond the grave,
    'Twill rise to an immortal birth.

"The hand that set it in the sky
    Shall make it brighter than before,
And sin's dark clouds or earth's thick storms
    Can hide its beauties nevermore."

" It is enough, my Lord," I cried :
    "Only this boon I ask for me :
That Thou wilt, when my course is run,
    Take me to share its joys with Thee."

LINES TO R——.

Sister, though around thy brow
  Twines no laurel of renown,
Yet in Heaven, even now,
  Waits for thee a golden crown—

Crown bedecked with many a gem
  Richer than Golconda's store;
He who wears such diadem
  Can no lack of wealth deplore.

Though at times thy way is hard,
  And thy pillow wet with tears,
Yet like thee the Savior fared—
  Had, like thee, His doubts and fears;

Saw at times the world's cold sneer,
  Felt stern persecution's sting,
Knew too well that in this sphere
  All was false and withering.

Yet He overcame the world,
  Conquered every fleshly lust,
All His foes to ruin hurled,
  And ascended to the Just.

And He promises to you,
  That He never will forsake,
But will guide you safely through,
  Till the promised rest you take.

Then take courage, sister, rise!
  Lift thy soul above all care;
Place thy hopes beyond the skies,
  Keep them firm by faith and prayer.

THE KILKENNY LEGEND.

Have you heard of the cats of Kilkenny?
    'Tis a wonderful story, indeed,
How two cats, old Dick and old Tommy,
    Were devoured by each at one feed.

'Tis said that a man of Kilkenny
    Heard a yawling outside his abode;
And he looked toward the place where he heard it,
    And saw a great dust in the road.

When the dust in the road had blown over,
    And a stop had been put to the wails,
The two cats were "ate up" entirely,
    Excepting a bit of their tails.

Now I think that these cats of Kilkenny
    Could not have performed such a task,
My reasons for doubting are many;
    One or two I will give if you ask.

Now, distrust against long-cherished notions,
    I am never inclined to be brewing;
But you know 'tis an unwise presumption,
    That a cat can devour without chewing;

Which must be the case with Kilkenny,
    The way that the story's proposed;
For before either cat could be swallowed,
    The jaws must be broken or closed.

Our argument was to convince you,
    Though I'm certain my first would avail,
A cat that could eat up another,
    Would not stop for a bit of the tail.

But, although this Kilkenny story
    Is not true, as a matter of fact,
The case is quite common, however,
    For parties of men thus to act.

For instance, two men have a quarrel,
    And endeavor to settle by law;
They will work at each other in trial
    Till they fall into poverty's maw.

Two women, who live near each other,
    Will often get into a brawl,
And fight with the weapons of slander
    Till others are roused by their yawl.

When their words of abuse are all over,
    And the neighborhood cleared of the spat,
They are found in the maw of dishonor
    Sunk as low as a Kilkenny cat.

And generally, when there is a conflict,
    Both parties of reason are cleft,
And worse than the cats of Kilkenny,
    Fight on till there's not a bit left.

CONFESSION HYMN. (s. m.)

I've been a wayward child,
    I've suffered sorrow's pain,
Through sin's dark valleys, drear and wild,
    My weary way has lain.

My wrongs I now deplore;
    The Savior's grace I've sought;
He bade me go and sin no more;
    His blood my ransom bought.

There's one thing left to do,
    That I may happy live;
I must unto my brethren go,
    And ask them to forgive.

Perhaps they'll be severe,
    And, in their righteous zeal,
Will turn from me a listening ear,
    Till I more deeply feel.

It may be, after all,
    When I to them shall go,
They'll think how apt they are to fall,
    And pity for me show.

At least, 'twill do no harm
    To give them such a chance;
It may their prejudice disarm,
    And my own joys enhance.

CONTENTMENT.

In that fair land beyond the sea,
    Where Ishmael's children roam at will,
There dwelt within a Moslem tower,
    An Emir, famed for lore and skill.

And often to his palace-home,
　Where wealth had all its splendor wrought,
The wise from other climes would come,
　To do him homage and be taught.

He made no boast of magic art,
　But gave to Allah all the praise,
And daily prayed that He'd impart
　New strength to walk in wisdom's ways.

One day there came within the court,
　A man who seemed quite ill at ease ;
He wished to know what he should do,
　To rid himself of his disease.

He did not ask increase of store ;
　His health was good, his friends were kind;
The prophet promised all he craved—
　He wanted a contented mind.

" Go," said the Emir, " find a man
　Who has this noble gift of mind,
And buy an under-robe of him,
　If to such traffic he's inclined."

The nabob thanked him for the word,—
　Then calling up his fav'rite gray,
He bade adieu to those he loved,
　And soon was speeding on his way.

But search was vain, no matter where,
　Through quiet lane or crowded street,—
All said a thing that was so rare,
　He never could expect to meet.

At last he heard—oh! joyful news!—
    Where dwelt the man he longed to see;
He lived contented, it was said,
    Although he was of low degree.

"Allah be praised," the nabob said,
    As to his course he·quickly flew;
As flies the eagle when he sees
    The prey he seeks recede from view.

Nor halted he, save to inquire,
    Till he had reached the poor man's cot.
And made his errand known to him.
    Which, strange to say, he granted not.

" Oh, give me this!" the nabob cried,
    " Here, take this gold, 'tis sordid pelf!"
" I would, by Allah," he replied,
    " But I've no shirt to wear myself!"

TO MY SINGER.

I have listened, dear Luc, to thy rapturous song,
    Of the beautiful isles far away o'er the sea,
And it cheers me to think that it will not be long
    Ere those islands of beauty receive you and me.

And the rich mellow tones of thy voice made me think
    Why it was that such power to a mortal was given; .
But we're sure the Creator intended to link
    By such charming attractions our earth to His heaven.

For we know beyond doubt that our blessings of peace
    Are directly bestowed from the Eden above,
And 'tis equally plain that joys must increase
    And become purer still near the fountain of love.

May thy future, fair maiden. be fraught with good deeds,
    Cheering hearts that are lonely and dark with despair,
And the God who remembers the poor in his needs
    Shall acknowledge and bless thee for service so rare.

TO JANE.

Dear Jane, your name has charms for me,
    'Tis sweeter far than any
Of those pet names that girls assume,
    As Peggie, Mollie, Jennie.

There's quite a fashion now abroad
    In country and in city
Of changing off those good old names
    For those that seem more pretty.

There's Cath'rine Jones, as large a girl
    As I have ever seen ;
She wants her name to Kittie changed,
    And says the folks are mean,

Because they will not call her so—
    She hates that " Catharind ;"
'Twill do for widows and old maids,
    Whose tastes are less refined.

I've sometimes thought that it would do,
    If men were so inclined,
To try to work a slight reform
    In matters of this kind;

So that the children might not look
    Upon their name with dread,
And wish their parents wiser were,
    Or they themselves were dead.

For instance, there is Peggy-Ann—
    Maria-Antoinette,
And Ada-Ida-Rosa-Bell,
    And step-and-fetch-it Bet.

But I must stop or some will say,
    " Keep still about this matter
Of finding fault with other folks,
    Your talk is only chatter.

" For if you'd children of your own
    To educate and name,
They'd likely suffer greatly more
    Than those of whom you blame."

TO WILL M. CARLETON.

Carleton, alone thou standest here,
    No kindred spirit dwells with thee;
For thou hast left thy native sphere,
    To wander, like the eagle, free,
And soared to realms before unsought
By those of weaker nerve and thought.

He mounts, with pinions strong, to dare
    The storm-king in his fiercest wrath,
With eye that quails not in the glare
    Of burning suns that cross his path,—
And thou, like him, with magic skill,
Canst wing those dizzy heights at will.

And sometimes, like the eagle, too,
    When, sated with celestial bliss,
He leaves his sphere of azure blue,
    To revel for a while in this,
Dost thou vouchsafe to bend thy wing
The words and acts of men to sing.

O, noble bard! whose matchless lyre
    Thy compeers imitate in vain,
May God thy deepest thoughts inspire.
    And sanctify thine every strain,
And to thy gifted mind impart
The graces of a Christian heart.

A MICHIGAN COURT SCENE.

In Michigan, some years ago,
    When everything was new and strange,
When honest men were all the go,
    And roughs were had, just for a change:

When doctors carried saddle-bags,
When preachers rode astride their nags.
When God would deign to meet His people
In a log church without a steeple;—

When lawyers and judges both were few ;
And, what may seem more strange to you,
They couldn't be bought for sums untold,
(Office would fail as well as gold) ;

A court scene took place which I will describe,
 (Though in description I often fail),
Where the court was held at a private house,
 And a log barn answered for a jail;

The presiding judge was a cross-eyed man,
 As jolly and free as you wish to meet;
Though he looked as grave as a deacon's mule,
 When he spoke to the culprit, near his feet.

" You have been condemned by the court," said he,
 " As being one of the meanest of men ;
For you took from his home at dead of night,
 The son of an old and respected hen.

" You are large enough to steal a sheep,
 Or back a quarter of an ox,
But instead of that, you sneaked around
 And carried away one of Jones' cocks.

" Now, for this crime, you may roost three days
 On the highest beam of our county jail;
So be off at once without any words,
 Your cackling and crowing will not avail."

They were taking him to his roosting place,
 When a voice called out from amidst the crowd,
" You have served him right, old gimlet-eyes,
 And you are a judge of whom we are proud."

"Who dares to enter here," said the judge.
   "And on our dignity intrude?"
"'Tis this old hoss," a voice replied,
   "Though 1 didn't mean to be quite so rude."

"You didn't ,hey! we'll attend to your case.
   And teach you manners, the best we are able,
Here, Brown, return as soon as you can,
   And lead this *old hoss* off to the stable."

LINES TO FANNIE.

We have met, dearest Fannie, some three times or more,
   And, according to custom, we strangers should be;
But I think on reflection that were it three-score,
   It would make little change in my friendship for thee.

There is much to observe, in the promise of mind,
   That is worthy of notice and careful inspection;
For in searching creation all through you will find
   No two persons alike in their mode of reflection.

Some are deep, dark and subtle; their channel of thought
   Runs in labyrinths fearful and strangely abstruse,
Like the caverns and caves which old ocean has wrought,
   Where the howling charybdis takes up its recluse.

Others seem like the fountain of crystal that flows
   From the midst of the throne where the sanctified
     tread;
So transparent and bright do its waters appear,
   That an angel might mirror himself in its bed.

And it seemed, gentle girl, as I sat by thy side,
 That thy mind was as pure as that fountain of bliss;
And it would have been pleasure with thee to abide,
 Had enjoyment alone been consulted in this.

TO MARTHA.

"Martha, thou'rt cumbered with much care,
 Thou takest life too hard."
Thus said the Master, while on earth,
 And thus repeats thy bard.

The bards, or poets, as they're called,
 Have struck with magic sound
Their lyre strings oft to others' names;
 To thine no notes resound.

But thou art faulty in the way
 Of having much to do;
Yet I prefer thee for my guide,
 To those whose cares are few.

And though upon thy lofty brow
 No coronet is placed,
No sparkling diamonds grace thy hands,
 No jewels gird thy waist;

Yet what are these, and songs of praise,
 To the real worth thou hast;
Honors and wealth shall pass away,
 But thy good works shall last.

BLINDNESS.

Struck blind! oh, God! is it a crime
    To wish that I had ne'er been born?
Or, being born to such a fate,
    To ask of reason to be shorn?

Or, what is better far than this,
    Or that which seems so, now, to me,
To pray Thee to receive my soul,
    And set this troubled spirit free?

I've stood beneath affliction's rod,
    And borne its lashings many a year,
Without a murmur of complaint,
    So far as other men could hear.

But Thou, whose all-observing eye
    Piercest my soul's dark resting place,
And seest the grief that lingers there
    The joys of time can ne'er efface;

Whose ear has heard each secret sigh,
    To Thee alone for help I look!
I tell thee, Maker, I must die,
    My soul this darkness cannot brook.

SEQUEL.

O, Father of Eternal Love!
    Thy grace deserves new praise each day!
For thou dost all things for the best,
    Regardless of what man may say;

Else, when I murmured at my fate,
　　And cursed with each returning breath,
The precious life Thou gavest me,
　　Thou hadst not kept my soul from death.

When first this cloud of darkness came
　　And filled my soul with doubts and fears;
I saw no avenue to light,
　　No hope within the coming years;

And, thinking that all chance was gone
　　Of being useful in this sphere,
I deemed it better to depart,
　　Than be a helpless burden here;

But, since that time, my mind has changed
　　From sadness to a cheerful mood;
For I've been taught that there are none
　　So weak that they can do no good;

And if the mind be thus employed
　　From day to day in others' weal,
It will be strengthened by each task,
　　And soon its sorrows cease to feel.

Another lesson I have learned,
　　Which gives me much encouragement,
Is this: Wherever ills are found,
　　Some compensation, too, is sent.

And this ameliorative gift
　　In many ways effects the blind;
But best of all, it has the power
　　To warm and elevate the mind.

And now, O Lord, I ask of Thee,
　　If Thou art pleased to hear this prayer,
That Thou wilt sanctify my heart,
　　And keep a thankful spirit there;

And when the King of Glory comes,
　　And turns all darkness into light,
And takes His people to Himself,
　　Then bless me with immortal sight.

LINES ADDRESSED TO MY AUNT.

(BY HER REQUEST.)

My dearest aunt, would I could grant
　　The little boon you ask of me;
I'd sing a song, in numbers long,
　　And this is what my theme should be:

I would not sing of man's exploits—
　　His deeds of cruelty and shame;
His mad career in search of wealth—
　　His love of power—his thirst for fame;

A nobler theme than these, I'd ask
　　Should thrill the lyre-strings of my heart,
I'd sing of woman's matchless love—
　　Her tender care—her wondrous art.

I'd tell of all her woes and wrongs—
　　How oft deceived—how sadly tried—
Her many struggles to be free—
　　Her plans for good, by sin defied.

And when I'd sung of all these things,
 That seem so wondrous strange to me,
I'd ask my muse to pause awhile,
 That I might sing, my aunt, to thee;

I'd sing of when affliction's hand
 Smote from my eyes the light of day;
And from my heart crushed every hope,
 That lingered there to cheer the way.

Thou, like a spirit, heaven-born,
 Freed from the Eden home above,
And hither sent by His command
 (Whose doings are all fraught with love),

Came to my aid, and with a wand
 That scattered darkness far away,
Pointed me upward to the sky,
 Where reigns an everlasting day.

A day so fair that in its light
 No mists can come, nor clouds arise
To cast a shadow on the soul,
 Or dim the lustre of the skies.

O! Aunt, whate'er our lot may be
 While we shall journey here below,
May this sweet hope inspire our hearts,
 Above no sorrow can we know.

And in that bright, eternal realm,
 Where none of sickness e'er complain,
The lame shall walk, the deaf shall hear,
 The blind receive their sight again.

LINES TO MY COUSIN.

Matilda, from thy early youth,
    Till now, some twenty years or more,
I've felt for thee a brother's love,
    And brooded all thy sorrows o'er.

I saw the dawning of thy mind,
    As to its course it slowly bent,
Like the fair moon, whose struggling beams
    Comfort and cheer where'er they're sent.

And when, in childhood's happy hours,
    You sported gaily round my knee,
I watched you with an inward pride,
    Well pleased that you were fond of me.

And when, in after years, I'd roamed
    O'er mountains wild and desert plain,
In my vain search for fame and wealth,
    And homeward turned my steps again,

With naught to show for all I'd done
    And suffered in those distant lands,
But pallid face and blinded eyes,
    And trembling limbs and palsied hands,

I heard again thy welcome voice;
    Again I felt thy warm embrace;
I knew by these, that thou wert true,
    Although I could not see thy face.

Ah! 'tis the soul, it is the soul
    That sees, perceives, and understands;
It speaks its language in the eyes,
    And in the voice, and through the hands.

The soul, whose value is so great
  That He around whose jasper throne
Seraphs and angels meekly bow,
  And all the spheres submission own,

Gave up the splendors of His court,
  His majesty and high estate,
To wrest it from the spoiler's power,
  His cunning snares and fiery hate,

Shall see the dawning of "that day
  For which all other days have been,"
And hear the notes of jubilee
  That free a ransomed world from sin;

And, seeing, hearing, feeling all .
  That God bestows with quickened power,
Like an imprisoned bird set free,
  Shall wing its flight to Eden's bowers.

But since that time I've stronger grown;
  Health has returned, and sorrow fled;
For, though I'm blind, without a home,
  And all the hopes of youth are dead,

I've learned to look, with eye of faith,
  Beyond the clouds of earth's cold night,
To that bright realm for saints prepared,
  Where all is joy, and love, and light.

And when a few more years have sped,
  And we have reached that shining shore,
We'll sit us down beside that throne,
  And talk our earthly trials o'er.

Then we shall see, as God now sees,
 That all these things are for the best,
And every wintry wind that blows
 But wafts us onward to our rest.

TO ELLEN.

Ellen, or, rather, Cousin Nell,
 If all the muses should conspire
To cast o'er me their sweetest spell,
 I'd strike for thee the magic lyre.

I would not say, in empty song,
 That thou wert graceful, gay and fair;
To dwell on these would do thee wrong
 When thou hast graces far more rare.

No, I would touch another string,
 A purer, nobler strain than this;
Like those glad themes that angels fling
 O'er harps of gold in realms of bliss.

The story of good actions wrought,
 Not for the joy the donors feel,
But sacrifices God has taught
 Should be endured for other's weal.

To those who thus resign their ease,
 That others happier may be,
Christ says, " As ye have done to these,
 So have ye done it unto me."

And, Ellen I have marked thee well,
    And seen the efforts thou hast made
The woes of others to dispel,
    While grief within thy bosom preyed.

And in that realm beyond the sun
    Where good works shall rewarded be,
I trust the plaudit of "well done"
    Shall be awarded unto thee.

CUPID AMONG COUSINS.

Fair Ellen, my cousin, I've met girls by the dozen,
    Whose faces and forms seemed with beauty replete;
And times without measure, I've had the sweet pleasure
    Of listening to voices entrancingly sweet;

Ah! now you are guessing the truth I'm confessing;
    You're changing your color; there's a witch in your eye;
But I can't help singing this song, though the ringing
    Of your merry laugh is re-echoed on high.

Then list while I tell ye how once it befell me
    To get into love with a fairy-like elf,
So like you in feature and mind was the creature,
    That any who saw her would say 'twas yourself.

'Tis said that whatever I plan I am never
    Disposed to forsake, while the least chance remains;
So, planning to marry this sprightly young fairy,
    I spared in the matter no labor nor pains.

And I might have succeeded; for 'twas just what I needed,
  And the sprite herself saw the thing in the same light;
But it grieves me to mention there arose a prevention,
  That thwarted my plans, and put all hope to flight.

'Twas said by wiseacres and crafty match-breakers,
  That generally cousins consenting to wed,
Will find the arrangement a source of estrangement,
  As the children of such ones had better be dead.

Thus, told that 'twas treason 'gainst mankind and reason,
  We gave up our project without more ado,
Concluding 'twas better ourselves not to fetter,
  Where such direful results were like to ensue.

Though sometimes, like Adam, and Eve, our grand-madam,
  While looking back sadly o'er what they had lost,
I regret I'd not tried the bright wall to o'erstride,
  And take the position regardless of cost.

But the sword is still swinging round that Eden, and
    ringing
  Like the death-knell of ages; there falls on the ear
The same stern prohibition, giving manumission
  From no law of nature, whether mild or severe.

THREE INDUCEMENTS TO LABOR.

I.

Some work for wealth, and some for power,
  And some to pass the time away;
But, as for me, I do confess
  That all these things inspire my lay.

That I want wealth, I don't deny;
　　I'd be like Crœsus, if I could;
With this exception: I would try
　　To spend my means in doing good.

Just think of all that wealth can bring.
　　'Tis like an Archimedian lever,
To elevate the moral world
　　And all its bands of evil sever.

 t gives the architect his power
　　To build the church and lofty steeple;
It pays the preacher for his work;
　　It warms the house, and clothes the people.

Without it we should lack the bread,
　　Which heaven vouchsafes from day to day;
With this condition on our part—
　　That we shall work as well as pray.

'Tis true, the Master said, while here,
　　"Beloved, shun the rich man's fate.
The needle's eye camels may pass
　　Easier than he through Heaven's gate!"

But then, 'tis said the needle's eye
　　Was but a gate, an entrance way,
Where camels, burdenless and bowed
　　Entered the city day by day.

So with the rich man, if he tries,
　　While traveling onward in life's road,
He'll find along the dusty way
　　Good use for all that Heaven's bestowed;

And, spending thus his surplus means,
> Till he has reached the Heavenly state,
He'll meekly lay his burdens down,
> And bow himself within the gate.

Then why should I not seek for wealth,
> When so much good may from it rise;
Not as the miser, lacking bread,
> And barring entrance to the skies;

But, dealing justly with my God,
> And kindly, too, with those around,
I'll save enough of earthly goods
> To keep me from the pauper's ground.

II.

I seek for power, but not the kind
> For which ambitious minions start,
That fires the soul with selfishness
> And crushes goodness from the heart.

The power the tyrant has to make
> His fellow-man a servile slave,
And keep him there beneath his yoke,
> Is not the power that I would

I'd rather strike the fetters off,
> And say to man, "Arise! be free!
From every chain that binds thee down,
> I charge thee, take thy liberty!"

The banners of reform should wave
> O'er hill and dale, the earth around;
The song of jubilee go up,
> Till all mankind should hear the sound.

The power I crave is not brute force;
    It lies within the realm of thought;
'Tis not of earth, but heaven-born,
    And by it, all good works are wrought.

It is the power that manhood feels
    When laboring in the cause of right;
It laughs at persecution's rage,
    And turns its hellish foes to flight.

It is the same that Luther had
    When, like a lion from his den,
He sallied forth from convent walls,
    To fight with devils and with men.

Contending always for the right,
    Opposing wrong in every place,
It yields to no vain compromise
    That would the cause of truth disgrace.

The boon I ask is not that Fame
    Would place on me her golden mead;
But power to save myself from sin,
    And aid a brother in his need.

III.

I'd work to pass the time away,
    If other motives there were none;
For more than half the ills of life
    Are in the idler's vineyard grown.

The ancient maxim still in use,
    Has often proved itself too true,
That "Satan finds some mischief still
    For any idle hands to do."

THE OASIS OF LIFE.

There are bright sunny spots in the desert of life,
    Far away from confusion and care,
And the pilgrim and stranger, dejected and worn,
    May at times find a resting-place there.

'Tis a beautiful sight for the languishing eye,
    As it turns from its sorrowing gaze,
On the darkness and gloom of life's dull, arid waste,
    To the joys which this prospect displays.

'Tis a relic of Eden, this vision from God,
    Being left for our guidance and cheer ;
As the earnest or foretaste of future reward,
    To be given when Christ shall appear.

But the transports of joy which illumine the soul,
    As they come through these visions of time,
Are beyond the weak language of man to express ;
    To declare them would need the Divine.

If, when blinded by passion, and cumbered with care,
    As we are in our physical state,
We receive such impressions of glory as these
    What delight must translation await.

Then redouble thy speed, laggard Time, for thy flight,
    Will but hasten the coming of bliss ;
And the transcendent joys of eternity's sphere,
    Shall compensate for trials in this.

ADVERTISEMENT.

The author of this book, Harvey A. Fuller, who for a number of years has been lecturing with success upon different interesting subjects, will cheerfully respond to those who wish to secure his services as a lecturer. Arrangements can be made by addressing him at Hillsdale, Mich. Below are inserted a few

NOTICES OF THE PRESS.

From the Coldwater (Mich.) Republican, Saturday, Oct. 22d, 1870.

The Blind Lecturer, Mr. H. A. Fuller, a graduate of Hillsdale College, and who has succeeded in gaining a fine education despite the affliction of total blindness, will deliver a lecture at the M. E. Church in this city on Tuesday evening, Nov. 1, 1870, and also at Girard on Monday evening, Oct. 31. Subject—"How the Blind See." Mr. Fuller has already delivered this lecture in many of our large cities, where it has been well received, and where the press has universally spoken very highly of it. The Toledo *Blade* contains the following notice of it:

"He gives an account of the number of blind in this country compared with those of Europe, of the early efforts and final success of philanthropists to found asylums for their care and instruction; of the New York Institution for the Blind, of which he was a member. The manner of life, amusements and employments of its inmates show that they wish to become useful in society. The mirthful side of their life is most happily illustrated by sketches and incidents from his own and other's experience, which cannot fail to draw a laugh from the stoniest heart, and drive the blues from the bluest. Concerning their thoughts and feelings, his remarks are eloquent and touching, and will warm the hearts of all who could be moved to pity."

From the Sandy Creek News (Sandy Creek, Orange Co., N. Y.) March 15, 1872.

APOLOGY.—We intended to have spoken, in our last week's issue, of the lecture given at the Congregational Church by Mr. Fuller, the blind orator. His lecture was entitled, "What a Blind Man Saw Among the Stars." It was replete with information; and the minute details given of the heavenly orbs, distances from each other, etc., led the hearer to look with astonishment upon the man who had such a wonderful memory; for all of his lectures are delivered from memory, being impressed upon that organ by being read to him. His manner of speaking was easy, and oratory good. Our citizens seemed well pleased with the lecture, and we hope Mr. Fuller will favor us with another at no distant date."

From the Jefferson County Journal (Jefferson Co., N. Y.) Nov. 16, 1871.

We had the pleasure, last Sabbath evening, of listening to the blind lecturer, Mr. Fuller, at the Baptist Church in Mannsville. The church was crowded and the aisles were full of people who stood respectfully during the entire lecture. The subject was "Temperance," and it was handled in an original manner. Drunkenness was affirmed to be a crime. The man who took sufficient intoxicating drink to dim his reasoning or moral faculties was a criminal and guilty of murder. Not only is such a one a self-murderer, but he has made himself a dangerous man to society. The liquor may prompt him to kill a man in his mad frenzy. Where lies the responsibility of an act of murder committed by an inebriate at the time of his intoxication? When he slew his fellow-man, his brain was frenzied, and he was not entirely responsible. The responsibility goes back to the time when he voluntarily took the maddening liquor and placed himself under its power; then it was that he made himself a murderer. This view of the subject, it will be seen, when carried out, touches the subject of temperance in all its bearings; the responsibility of individual moderate drinkers and of the public for its opinion are vitally connected with it. The speaker's style was chaste and finished, and his address throughout betokened the scholar as well as the warm-hearted man. His pronunciation was almost faultless, his voice clear and distinct, and some portions of his address were remarkably fine and affecting, especially so were his parallel pictures of the home of the temperance man. We might give extracts from his address, but space will not permit, and we presume all of our readers will improve the opportunity of hearing him and receiving the benefit of his instructive lectures from his own lips. Mr. Fuller is apparently about thirty-five years of age. He was born in the town of Ellisburg, and lost the sight of one eye when a child; the other eye was destroyed by inflammation when he was about eighteen years of age, since which time he has been totally blind. He was for several years at the school for the blind in New York city; since then he has attended and graduated at Hillsdale College, paying the expenses of his education, in the main, as he went along. He is an example of what industry and perseverance can accomplish for one who has to contend against great disadvantages. He passed through his college course, learning his lessons by having some one read them to him, and graduated with honor. Since his graduation he has supported himself by lecturing, in which he has met with much success. He very seldom charges an admittance fee, but has a collection taken up at the close of his address, when all who appreciate his lecture and the cause in which he is engaged have an opportunity to contribute. Certainly the success he has met with, and the instructive and moral power of his lectures are emphatic in demonstrating that his choice has been wise in taking public speaking for his vocation. He has prepared and delivered lectures on several interesting topics, of which one of the most interesting is on the mode of instruction for the blind. His stay in this part of the country will probably be brief, so that all who are desirous of securing him to lecture in their vicinity, should make arrangements to secure his services at once. His lecturing through the country would be of great value to the cause of Temperance and morality.

NOTICE TO THE PUBLIC.

As I have been requested by Mr. Downey, who has had the charge of getting out the first edition of "Trimsharp's Account of Himself," (he knowing that I had read the whole work) to express my opinion of its merits, I most cheerfully comply with his request by saying that I have found the historical part to be exceedingly well written, giving many incidents in his own life, as well as in the lives of several others, who, like himself, were deprived of the blessing of sight, that will be found interesting to the general reader; and I am also satisfied that his Poems indicate such an adaptation of mind to that branch of writing, that it will be well for him to give it his particular attention. And I am willing to risk my reputation *as a judge of the wants of the people*, by saying that I have not a doubt of his meeting with great success in thus offering these reminiscences to an appreciative public.

A. W. CHASE, M. D.,

Prest. and Supt. of the Ann Arbor Printing and Publishing Company, Author of "Dr. Chase's Recipes; or, Information for Everybody," and "Dr. Chase's Family Physician, Farrier, Bee-Keeper, and Second Receipt Book."